Betty,

With love from Toni

FOUL CONTAGION

Toni Lilly

The Book Guild Ltd
Sussex, England

This book is a work of fiction. The characters and situations in this story are imaginary. No resemblance is intended between these characters and any real persons, either living or dead.

The Book Guild Ltd
25 High Street
Lewes, Sussex

First published 1998

Set in Baskerville

Typesetting by
Southern Reproductions (Sussex)
Crowborough, Sussex

Printed in Great Britain by
Antony Rowe Ltd
Chippenham, Wiltshire

A catalogue record for this book is
available from the British Library

ISBN 1 85776 355 6

For Cordelia, loving owner
of the original Rodrigo

1

Mrs Bloomfield, probably gentler and certainly less decisive than the average primary school headmistress, had often expressed doubts about the daily journal composition imposed upon the older children.

'Yes, I agree it's a way of training them to write lucidly,' she would twitter, fiddling with the chain that kept her reading glasses from straying too far afield, 'but doesn't it sometimes strike you as a kind of second-hand invasion of the parents' privacy? I mean, one does read the most extraordinary things at times.'

And how one did, thought Phoebe Fielding, imagining the reactions of Susie Johnson's family should they ever hear of the recent hilarity in the staffroom about Susie's habit of joining Mummy and Auntie Jean in their bed on Sunday mornings while Daddy slept in the spare room.

'I grant you they're under no obligation to write the truth,' Mrs Bloomfield went on pondering aloud, 'but then at that age how can they possibly know what would be best suppressed?'

'Well, as far as I'm concerned,' Mr Brooks, the peripatetic music teacher, put in with typical hearty abandon, 'the less they suppress the better. If one didn't occasionally get a spot of light entertainment round these parts one would go bonkers.'

'What I like about the journals,' Miss Seaton, the deputy head, said as she frowned repressively at him, 'is the insight they give us into the varying degrees of individual parent involvement. Wouldn't you say so, Phoebe?'

'I certainly would.'

Phoebe had looked down to hide a grin. The Watsons would probably both have strokes if they read their Elizabeth's innocent description of noises off which clearly indicated an orgy of unbridled sex on their part. On the other hand, while Phoebe simply didn't believe that Mrs Farquharson was in the habit of hobnobbing with the Duchess of Buccleuch, who had recently opened a Somerstrand sale of work, the social details in Joanna's diary were far too sophisticated to have been recorded by a ten-year-old unassisted.

It was Matthew Proctor who rather worried Phoebe. A warm-hearted little boy, cuddling up to her whenever he could without arousing ridicule from the others, he was plainly not getting his ration of affection at home.

'Try to look after Matthew a bit,' she had once said to Tracy Bennett, a motherly little girl; at least Phoebe was lucky in that none of her class was particularly tough. In fact Matthew had a perfectly decent mother of his own, but she was unassertive and young, only six or seven years older than Phoebe herself and a great deal younger than her husband. There the trouble needed little analysis. Matthew's father, a fair way up the social scale in comparison with most of the other Somerstrand parents in that he was the senior partner in the local branch of a national firm of accountants, was a domestic tyrant pure and simple. Her every encounter with him had made this increasingly clear to Phoebe and everything Matthew wrote confirmed it.

The *au pair* girl, Montse, to whom Matthew had evidently become greatly attached, had left abruptly after what the diary suggested must have been a quite unholy row – something to do with the paternal underpants having been permitted to appear in all their glory on the family clothes-line on a Sunday afternoon. And now, shortly before Christmas, Marmalade had been taken to the vet to be 'put to sleep'.

'But why?' Phoebe's arm encircled the weeping Matthew.

'Because he didn't get on with Humphrey' – a fat and

singularly unattractive standard poodle who had lifted his leg against several cars on the last Open Day.

'And then he scratched Daddy.'

Why too was what Phoebe would have liked to know.

'Daddy didn't like cats, you see.' Matthew's tears flowed afresh. 'But I loved Marmalade. And he wasn't at all old. Less than one. It isn't fair. I hate Daddy.'

Phoebe entirely saw his point.

2

On his retirement from one of the more humdrum branches of Birmingham's civil service Mr Binding had been anticipating a time of long-awaited peace and tranquillity – a spot of golf, a quiet Sunday lunch, not too indigestible, of course, at the George and Dragon, some gentle, unambitious gardening – lettuces and tomatoes, perhaps – while his wife occupied herself with suitable feminine occupations – the Somerstrand WI, the Oxfam shop, a little participation in church activities, the reassembly of old Christmas cards to be sold in aid of good causes, the collection of milk-bottle tops, used stamps and so forth – in fact everything his dear departed Mildred would have done.

Priscilla was his second wife, Mildred having succumbed while still in her fifties to some rare and unpronounceable blood disease, and though Mr Binding was really very fond of his new partner, there were times when he wondered uneasily what Mildred would have thought or, worse still, might be thinking.

The absolute antithesis of everything Mildred had been, Priscilla was a complete extrovert – untidy, undomesticated, careless of what the neighbours might say about the unmown lawn, the lack of paper doilies on the cake plates and, most alarming of all, addicted to the use of four-letter words which tended to ring out at their loudest on summer evenings when everyone was at home and the windows wide open.

Even so they never quarrelled, at least not until the arrival of Orestes, a large young ginger tom who had suddenly appeared out of the blue and, thanks to Priscilla's sporadic ministrations, decided to move in. To judge from his appetite and indislodgeability he belonged to nobody, though Mr Binding did try a surreptitious and fruitless advertisement in the local paper.

'It's the smell that's the worst,' he complained to Priscilla after the vicar's wife, looking pale, had cut short a visit and the window cleaner, wrinkling his nose and grinning broadly, had exclaimed, 'You have a tom! Or toms!'

'You'll have to have him neutered. That should stop it.'

Now where had he picked up that piece of information? he wondered. Mildred would never have tolerated a cat in the house.

'Of couse he'll have to be neutered, now that we know we can keep him,' Priscilla agreed warmly. 'Otherwise he'll wander and we may well lose him.'

'You know, I can't help suspecting I've seen that cat before,' Mr Cruikshank, owner of the Somerstrand veterinary practice, said thoughtfully a week later, eyeing the recumbent Orestes as he began to come round after the anaesthetic.

'Really?' commented his assistant, Tim Proud, only fairly recently qualified, with an uneasy glance at the pretty receptionist, who had turned faintly pink. 'Isn't he just a type? Most ginger toms look pretty similar, don't they?'

'Maybe, but I'm not convinced.' Mr Cruikshank shook his greying head. 'That beard. Those white whiskers. No, there's definitely something at the back of my mind. Some unpleasant associations, which is odd, as he's young and he comes from a good home. Still,' to the others' great relief he turned away from the half-open window, 'it will come to me sooner or later, you'll see.'

Both the young man and the girl devoutly hoped it would not.

3

Alison Edenfield had never regretted giving up nursing to open a boarding kennels, which she found a source of great personal satisfaction as well as the answer to a need which encounters with anxious dog-owning patients had shown her was a very real one. An added bonus was the end it brought to hospital night shifts, so disruptive to her family life.

To help her she employed two others - Pam, a somewhat disenchanted ex-secretary in her thirties with a genuine love of animals, and Jane, whom she couldn't help rather disliking and would probably have sacked had she dared.

The trouble there was that Harold, Jane's unsavoury boyfriend, was a transcontinental heavy goods driver, as was Rupert, Alison's husband, and both worked for the same Middlemoor fruit importers. Rupert was far older than Harold and a great deal better educated, but the roving life was what most appealed to him and that was all there was to it. Anyway there was something about Harold, some hint of menace, that made Alison wary of offending him. With a business depending so much on local goodwill, malicious comment from outside was the last thing she needed, and Rupert, whose very survival might depend on the correct responses of his vehicle, could well do without a hostile and unscrupulous colleague. So Jane stayed on.

This particular evening, while Rupert and his HGV would presumably be on the way home, somewhere between Rouen and Calais, and Harold back in Middlemoor for the next forty-eight hours, Alison cast an eye over the occupants of the various cages scattered in little blocks around the paddock, then returned to her office to deal with the day's paperwork.

Three dogs in today, two out and that wretched Mrs Sykes had rung from London to say her return was going to be delayed for a week just at a time when the kennels were already fully booked well in advance for an early Easter. That meant that someone would have to double up.

In the administration hut just off the office Jane was washing the evening's dog bowls, as sketchily as usual, no doubt. Pam, having worked through her lunch hour, had already gone home. In the house Alison's son and daughter with any luck would be getting on with their homework, television programmes permitting, of course.

It was about half past six when Clare Forrester appeared, come to collect her little dog, a 'day-boy' while she worked in an office in the town. Day-dogs were quite a feature of Alison's business.

'Hello,' she greeted Alison. 'It's pay day.' She handed over the weekly sum. 'How are things?'

'All right, I think,' Alison told her. 'Thanks, Clare. I'll come with you to get Rodrigo. He's over in the little run by himself. Pam seems to feel he's been a bit listless recently, so I suppose she thought he'd have more peace and quiet in there.'

'No need. I've already fetched him.' As a long-standing and trusted client, Clare was allowed to put him in and out unsupervised. 'He's in the car.'

'But he can't be.' Alison stared at her. 'I've just seen him in there and I never saw you come past.'

'Well no, because I didn't.' Clare too was surprised. 'He wasn't in the little run. He was in the one next to the gate. You can't have seen properly.'

'But I did!' Alison exclaimed. 'How can I not have? This is ridiculous. All right, you've got him in the car, but do just come over to that run with me. Do you mind?'

'OK,' Clare said soothingly and accompanied her to the furthest corner of the field.

'Look there then!' Alison pointed triumphantly to a kind of hutch at the end of a narrow enclosed run. 'There he is, surely? Fast asleep in the corner.'

Clare bent to peer closely at the little brownish-gold bundle curled up against the inner wall, half-encircled by what promised to become a bushy up-curling tail.

'But that's not Rodrigo. It's about as near a look-alike as you could get, but it isn't him. Anyway that one has to be younger, not more than a pup. Look at the tail.'

'M'm.' Alison's brow was furrowed. 'You're right, of course. That one's much younger. Stupid of me. It's just that I've never set eyes on that dog before. I know who we've got and I certainly didn't book him in. Here, boy!' She clapped her hands gently, and slowly the little creature stirred and unfurled himself to stand staring sleepily at them both.

'Heavens!' Clare drew in her breath sharply. 'Even the little black muzzle's like Rodsey's. But couldn't Jane or Pam have taken him in?'

'If they did, they didn't put it in the book. Besides, I've been here all day.' It would be the wretched Jane, of course, Alison thought, trying to make a bit for herself on the side; well, she'd have to do something about that later. And it would have been Jane who'd moved Rodrigo from where Pam had left him, so as to make room for the newcomer.

'Yes, it's really quite extraordinary how like Rodrigo he looks. I know Rods is a mongrel, but he's very unusual. You just don't see dogs like that round here.'

'You do in Barcelona,' Clare remarked. 'There are droves of them over there, just like that. By and large the ordinary Spanish don't seem to go in for distinct breeds the way we do. Oh, don't worry, Alison. There'll be an explanation. You're not hallucinating, if that's what you're thinking.'

But by now Alison could almost have wished she were.

'The Spanish?' she echoed, appalled. 'That dog's Spanish, is that what you're saying?'

'Well, I shouldn't be surprised. So what, though? Oh, I see.' She had caught Alison's line of thought. 'Of course. Jane's boyfriend. He came back from Barcelona a couple of days ago, didn't he?'

'You know about him then?'

'Main topic of conversation every time I give her a lift. She often comes off duty when I'm collecting Rods and her place is on my way home. I wouldn't put anything past him; he sounds a horror.'

'Exactly. And just right for Jane,' Alison said grimly. 'So, what are they up to? Why bring the pup here?'

'All too obvious, isn't it? When Harold was in Spain on his last trip he came across some British tourist or whatever from this area who'd got hold of the pup and wanted to bring it back, but didn't fancy paying for the six months' quarantine and all that goes with it – the journey, the carrier you have to have and so on. I know what it costs,' she added, grimacing. 'So for some far lesser amount dear Harold agreed to smuggle the pup through in his HGV. And it's here now because the tourist or whatever isn't back yet and Harold has nowhere to keep it till he arrives. At least that's what I'd guess.'

A silence followed, broken only by the usual sporadic barking and the clatter of Jane's bowls against the sink.

'This is frightful,' Alison said eventually. 'That unspeakable little bitch!' A strong word for her. 'If this comes out, I'll be ruined. Nobody will risk using the kennels for months. God, I wish Rupert were here!'

'Maybe it's as well he isn't. At least he'll have an alibi if there should be any trouble. Otherwise Harold might find it necessary to make out it was Rupert who did it.'

'Oh, Lord, so he might.' Alison was really shaken. 'And it would be Rupert's word against his. Clare, must you go right now? Could you come back to the office for a sherry and a think? Look,' she went on as they turned away, 'you've spent a long time in Spain. What would you reckon is the likelihood of that pup incubating rabies?'

From the look of her she needed that sherry pretty badly.

'Wildly unlikely, honestly. There wasn't any in Catalonia when I left about two years ago. All the dogs had to be vaccinated by law; in my village they were all done free at the town hall on a fixed date. I was quite badly bitten once and they said at the hospital that the only risk, very slight, was from bats. Just as long as it really was the Barcelona area,' she added. 'Can we be sure of that?'

'Yes, I think so.' Back in her office Alison opened a cupboard and brought out a bottle and two glasses. 'Rupert said something about that. Somebody was going to bring a consignment of oranges up from Valencia for Harold to collect there.'

'Still, quite apart from that you'll have to get the pup out of here pronto.'

'And I'll have to be careful about how I tackle accusing Jane. It could all be some awful mistake, though I don't see how. I'll need to give this one a bit of thought.'

She didn't have much time.

'Hi there, Alison!' Jane's free use of her first name always irked her much older employer. 'I'm just off now. See you tomorrow.' She nodded at Clare. 'I shan't need a lift tonight. Harold will be waiting for me outside.'

'All right. But Jane, just a minute before you go. That little brown pup over there in the far corner. Where has he come from, do you know? I've never seen him before this evening and there's no record of him in the book.'

'Oh.' Jane's expression changed to one of wary defensiveness. 'I wouldn't know. You could ask Pam tomorrow.'

'I could ring her up now. Should I, do you think? She said she was staying in tonight.'

'Up to you!' The girl shrugged. 'Well, I'll be off.'

'Not quite yet, if you don't mind,' said Alison. 'Someone – and not I – has done something irregular and no strangers have been alone on the premises. So it comes down to you or Pam and I'm quite prepared to ring her now, if you don't think it rather pointless. Either way I'm going to to get to the bottom of this.'

A blast on a car horn indicated that Harold was indeed waiting. Jane began to look rather desperate.

'What interests us,' Clare had decided it was time to take a hand, 'is that little dog's extraordinary resemblance to my Rodrigo, who came from Barcelona. And I gather that Harold has just returned from there.'

Another hoot.

'So if this has anything to do with him, don't you think you'd better say so?' pursued Alison. 'The sooner we know the truth the sooner we can do something to protect the kennels. Even you must know that it's a serious offence to smuggle an animal in from abroad.'

It was probably Harold's third hoot – that and the comparative mildness of Alison's tone – that finished Jane.

'All right, it's true,' she admitted sullenly, 'but I wasn't in on any of it. Harold just produced the dog and said I'd got to hide it here and I didn't know what else to do. I'm sorry, Alison. I knew he'd be in dead trouble if I gave him away and he scares me sometimes.'

'Then you'd do far better to part before you get any more involved with him. Clare, would you be very kind and ask him to come here for a minute? No, you stay here, Jane.'

Till then Clare had seen Harold from a distance only. Close to he was even less prepossessing – burly, greasy, not overclean and reeking of tobacco smoke.

'Mr Clitheroe,' Alison greeted him bravely, 'it's about that little Spanish dog you asked Jane to care for.'

'What?' Harold's already florid face reddened further and his too small grey eyes glinted nastily. 'I never. You never.'

The look he directed at Jane suggested to Clare that perhaps she would be needing a lift home after all.

'Sit down, Mr Clitheroe. Jane didn't give you away. I saw the pup and it was all too easy to work out.'

Still glaring, Harold sat.

'All right, I asked her to look after the dog for a few days and considering how little you pay her I didn't see why I should go buying dog food. But what d'you mean about Spanish? You can't prove nothing. The dog doesn't bark with a foreign accent, does it?'

'I've no doubt it could be proved if necessary.' Alison drew in a deep breath. 'Still, I'm not going to try it. What I really must know, though, is exactly what did happen. Where did you get that dog, and who's he for? Please.'

'Go on, Hal,' pleaded Jane rather pathetically. 'If she says she won't shop you, she won't. And I don't want to lose my job neither. I won't, will I, Alison?'

Reluctantly Alison shook her head. 'Oh, I suppose not, though you deserve to.' Glancing at the bottle, she reflected briefly on the tongue-loosening effects of sherry before deciding that there were limits to self-abasement. 'Though after this you'll probably be quite lucky to have a job not to lose.'

'So what's all the fuss about then?' demanded Harold a shade less truculently.

'The actual risk of rabies, which mercifully Miss Forrester thinks is fairly negligible in an animal from Catalonia. Plus the awful trouble we'll all be in if this ever comes out - you for what you did and I for my part in covering it up to save my whole livelihood. So come on now. We really have to have the full story.'

The three women stood waiting while a scowling Harold stood silent, plainly weighing up possible lines of defence.

'All right then,' he growled eventually. 'It was the other night in a little bar in Sitges, if you must know. There was an English bloke in there who could speak the lingo - Catalan, whatever - and seemed to know the boss. And he - the boss, that is - had a bitch that had recently had pups. They'd been weaned and was running all over the place pissing and shitting and getting under people's feet and so they was going to have to go to the pound in Barcelona. And as you'll have realized from that one over there, they was pretty little brutes. So this English fellow asked me if I'd bring one home for him to give his girlfriend when she came back from some trip. He knew what I did, see; we'd been talking all evening. And he lived not too far from here - Sunderland, I think it was, or maybe Gateshead. He gave me fifty quid and he managed to get hold of a couple of pills to keep the pup quiet on the journey. Nothing to it, really.'

'But why go to such lengths?' Alison was exasperated. 'Surely he knew the risk you'd both be running? And for fifty pounds he could have had the choice of any number of pretty British mongrels!'

'Oh, you know how it is.' Harold shrugged. 'We'd been drinking all evening. We had thick heads the next day, but by then he'd given me the cash and the bloke in the bar had handed over the pup, so we just went on with it.'

'And now the damage is done,' said Alison. 'I shan't say anything to anyone, but there's no way I can keep the poor little thing here. You'll have to take him with you tonight.'

'Here, hold on!' Harold was affronted. 'You know I've nowhere to keep it. Besides, I'm hardly ever here.'

'Jane then.'

'I can't take him,' she protested. 'I live in a fourth-floor bedsit. I haven't room for a canary. Couldn't you possibly, Clare?'

'Oh, don't be silly.' Clare glanced irritably at her watch. Jane and Harold had already cost her forty minutes and Paul was expecting her for supper. 'And bring him back here every day along with Rods? You'll just have to think of something yourselves.'

'Yes, and before you go,' Alison put in as, sighing resentfully, Harold rose and headed for the door, 'I've got to know about this man. What did you arrange with him about collecting the dog?'

'He'll be coming here,' Jane told her glumly. 'Somehow – don't ask me how – I was to keep him out of your way for the next ten days till the bloke got back from Spain.'

'So what's his name? He's from Sunderland, you said?'

'Yeah, or maybe Gateshead. It's Bert Rollins. Or Robbins.'

Harold must certainly have been pretty drunk.

'Right then.' Alison had the last word. 'You go now and collect the pup. And when Bert Rollins or Robbins comes I'll give him your address, Mr Clitheroe, or whatever address Jane lets me know will find the pup. And a piece of my mind!'

When Rupert arrived home late next evening, tired and welcoming the prospect of a couple of days' peace with his family, he was horrified to hear what had happened.

'Of all the criminal idiocy!' he raged. 'Drugs one might have expected from Harold. At least that would have netted him something. But a pup! To risk his own job and a thumping fine, as well as putting our business in jeopardy, all for a miserable fifty pounds. It makes one vomit. Just wait till I see him!'

'I wouldn't say too much if I were you,' Alison advised. 'Obviously drink had a lot to do with it, but it's been dealt with and he could be a bad enemy. And be careful never to mention it in front of the children. So long as they know nothing about it they can't let anything slip. But I must say,' she pushed a strand of hair back from her overheated face, 'I do object to being turned into a second-hand criminal!'

Still, there was no point in putting further pressure on her husband to abandon the road for the administrative job in his firm's office open to him whenever he cared to take it - an option most certainly not available to Harold.

'Another two years, and I'll pack it in,' was what he always said.

And of course there were some quite useful perks that he would lose if he did. By now he and Alison had a well-stocked cellar, acquired quite legitimately over successive trips, and the storeroom was filled with dried fruit, nuts, olives, small tins of exotic fish regularly picked up very cheaply from a large supermarket just into Spain, not to mention rather more expensive French delicacies. Alison never actually resold them, but a certain amount of polite barter with dog food suppliers and other contacts helped considerably to keep down her running costs.

'I'm a bit worried about that other man, though,' she fretted. 'You'll have gone again by the time he arrives, but I can't let him get clean away with it without saying something. I just hope he won't turn nasty.'

'I doubt very much if he'll come now,' Rupert encouraged her. 'Presumably Harold won't be able to contact him, but surely he'll get onto Jane to try to fix a time when you aren't likely to be around and she'll put him off.'

'I suppose so, with any luck,' Alison agreed gloomily. 'Because it's too much to hope that Clare will be here at the right moment again. She was an enormous help with Harold.'

Rupert nodded. 'She's a good girl. She must be adaptable, because it must seem strange to her living here after all that time in Spain. Where did you say her parents hang out?'

'Somewhere down south, I believe. But she must have been up here for quite a while now. Rodrigo's been coming to us for over a year.'

A couple of days later Rupert was off again, this time for Toulouse, and six days after that, during the middle of the afternoon, he was proved wrong.

Alison and Pam were in the paddock with Rodrigo, trying to coax him into showing a little more animation.

'You know, I really am beginning to get worried about him,' Alison was saying. 'He just isn't the dog he was when he first came. He's so up-and-downish. One day he's leaping about like a mad thing, the next he's an absolute zombie. And he's not even five yet. There has to be something wrong.'

'Clare said he was sick in the night,' Pam commented. 'Apparently he quite often is. She's probably told you about her arrangement with the local butcher for offcuts and so on, and now she's wondering whether he could be allergic to fresh meat.'

'He really should go to the vet.'

'He's always going to the vet, more than one actually, because of the different ones who do emergencies on Sundays. But somehow it never seems to help him for long. If he isn't being sick, he's limping or having diarrhoea or growling at strangers in a way he never did before. It must be costing Clare a fortune.'

'Excuse me.' The stranger standing behind them must have found the main gate unpadlocked – Jane again, of course – and had let himself in without even ringing the bell. 'Forgive me for coming in working hours, but I was hoping for a word with Jane.' His manner and the uncertainty of the smile that wavered between the two women brought it home suddenly to Alison that he would have no means of knowing whether or not Pam were Jane. Harold was unlikely to have thought of providing a physical description.

With a sudden burst of fury, fuelled by her anxiety over Rodrigo, she decided to give him a run for his money.

'She isn't here at the moment,' she said blandly. 'In fact she's on holiday for the next fortnight.' Should Jane appear inopportunely, she resolved, she was going to be 'Sarah' and like it. 'Is there anything I can do for you?'

'No, no, I don't think so.' Patently at a loss, he shook his head. 'Are you sure? I mean, that's to say I understood quite definitely that she'd be here.'

'Well, I should know.' Now Alison's rage was so very near the surface that Pam for one could sense it. 'I'm her employer. These are my kennels.'

'I see.' With dawning comprehension the stranger looked increasingly uneasy. 'And she's left no message for me?'

'No, no message. Nor a pup either, Mr Robbins. Or is it Rollins? Your friend Mr Clitheroe didn't seem too sure. Nor did he seem to grasp the enormity of what you've both done, conspiring to bring a foreign dog into the country in defiance of all the quarantine regulations. If you come to my office, I'll give you Jane's address, where no doubt you'll find her out of working hours. And you can count yourself lucky that I haven't reported you to the police!'

Perhaps it was a mistake to bring the police into it – that or the admission that she wasn't going to them. At any rate the man abruptly dropped all pretence of politeness and stepped forward to grasp her by the arm.

'Now just a minute, lady. You come off it. Where's that pup then? You haven't done anything to it, have you? Because I paid for it, you know.' To emphasize the point he gave the arm a vigorous shake. 'All of fifty quid. What about that then?'

At which point Rodrigo, who loved Alison only a little less than Clare, roused himself from his torpor and, as he would have done in the past in such circumstances, bit him well and truly in the calf.

4

For Tim Proud it had been a long, hard day, a good deal harder than the average, and in no way improved by the absence of Mr Cruikshank, currently recovering at home from the effects of a kick from a cow. Happily – though Tim had slightly mixed feelings about quite how happily – it had been a very long-range kick and a lot less damaging than it might have been.

Still, enough was enough. Tim's score so far, morning and midday surgeries apart, was a colic-stricken horse on a farm seven miles away, another in quite the opposite direction requiring to be gelded, a litter of mysteriously non-doing piglets and three dogs whose owners were affluent, lazy or concerned enough to pay for a home visit.

And now as, more than thankfully, he was nearing the end of evening surgery, the last pair he would ever have chosen to see again – Ivy Miller and her Fritz – were ushered into his presence.

'It's them sores again, Mr Proud,' she stated reproachfully. 'They're as bad as ever. That powder you gave me for him didn't do any good, at least not for long it didn't. Just take a look.' With a heave she raised the middle-aged dachshund onto the surgery table, hastily wiped down after the last patient, and lifted both ears to display the familiar sight he most dreaded – two large and angry sores on the underside of each.

'They're as big as a ten pence piece.' She was right; if anything it was an understatement. 'Can't you really think of anything that could be causing it?'

The dreadful thing was that Tim could not. Nor could Mr Cruikshank when previously consulted by him. Frankly they were baffled. According to the records, Ivy had brought Fritz to the surgery sixteen times during the last six months, an appalling expense for someone who earned her living cleaning other people's houses, and still it had been impossible to restore him to anything approaching complete health for more than the odd week in the course of a string of various ailments which might or might not be connected.

'Some kind of allergy to sunlight?' Cruikshank had suggested.

'In Somerstrand?' Tim had been stung into retorting. So far it had been a particularly dismal spring. 'And in any case, why the underside of the ears? Wouldn't you have expected it to be the outer? And why the symmetry? It's weird.'

'What's more,' Ivy persisted now, 'this last week or two he's been acting a bit as if he was blind. Only for a few seconds at a time, mind, so I could be wrong. But it's happened several times and my Ned's noticed it too.'

'Oh dear.' Tim peered closely at the melancholy brown eyes. 'They look all right. He certainly isn't blind now.'

'No, not now, I grant you. But that's not to say it didn't happen, nor that it won't happen again. He isn't happy in himself neither; well, how could he be? Gets real crotchety at times, and he used to be so good-tempered.'

'Well, I'll give him another injection,' Tim told her now, 'but I might as well be honest and confess that it beats me. I've never seen a case like this. All we can do, I think, is refer him to the veterinary hospital at Exleigh. It's a longish way, but if we can get him an appointment we can try to organize some form of transport for him.'

Cruikshank and he did at least owe her that, he felt, as she sniffed indignantly, picked up Fritz and departed.

The last patient was Colonel Power's beagle, Dreyfus, suffering from an infected anal gland which involved a certain amount of what must have been painful squeezing on Tim's part and furious resistance from Dreyfus, who had to end up with a jaw-restricting bandage.

'Steady on, old boy,' urged the Colonel, struggling valiantly at that end, while Tim dealt with the swelling at the other. 'Soon be over. Blasted nuisance, these things, you know,' he added.

'I know,' Tim agreed wearily, 'but at least one can do something about them.'

The Colonel, an elderly widower, shot a shrewd glance at Tim, who had grown up in Somerstrand and whom he had known since his early teens.

'There's something wrong, isn't there? More than Cruikshank being out of action. You look all in.'

'I am a bit,' Tim confessed. 'It's that dog of Ivy Miller's,' and to his own surprise and mild shame he found himself telling the Colonel all about it.

Time was passing; at one stage there was a gentle knock as Angela's head appeared around the door.

'All right if I go now? I've locked everything up and I've got a date.'

'OK. Good night and have fun,' Tim answered mechanically and, more relaxed now, went on with the saga.

The Colonel was one of the most practical, down-to-earth characters he had ever encountered and would never have dreamt of betraying a confidence. Freed from his bonds and relieved of pain now, Dreyfus had flopped on the floor between them.

'Well, I don't know,' said the Colonel at last, feeling in his pocket for his pipe. 'Tell me about this Ivy Miller. What's her history? She or the dog ever been abroad?'

'I've no idea.' Tim was surprised at the question. 'I shouldn't think so. Certainly not the dog; he came from a breeder near Calne. Ivy might have had the odd package holiday, I suppose. You must know her. She's the Proctors' daily. Lives at the end of Jubilee Crescent.'

'Oh, her. The fattish one with red hair and the shopping trolley.'

'That's right. But what are you driving at?'

'Nothing really. Just that if this had been the Sudan forty years ago, after all you've just told me I shouldn't have had the slightest doubt about it. Primmer's disease.'

'What's that?' A faint recollection of something once read in a textbook surfaced to niggle at Tim's brain, but not enough to be pinned down and identified.

'It's a parasitic thing. Carried in the first instance, they said, by sandflies in hot inland regions, especially where there's stagnant water around. Animals get it mostly, not so much cattle and pigs because of their hides, but dogs particularly.'

'Humans too?'

'Oh yes, quite often in the more rundown areas where they weren't too good on hygiene and the flies were thickest. It was the children who were most at risk, though adults could get it too. I had a friend, an MO, who used to talk about it a lot. Can't say I ever encountered a case myself. But the danger wasn't just from the sandflies, you see. Once a person or animal had contracted the damned thing he could pass it on through various forms of contact.'

'Such as?'

'Oh, body fluids; dogs get up to some pretty filthy things, don't they? Or by touching lesions. By the way, I take it you washed your hands after dealing with that dachshund?'

'Lord, yes!' Tim gesticulated towards a sink in the corner. 'Any other symptoms you can remember?'

'Not offhand.' The Colonel thought hard for a few moments. 'Oh well, yes; hair loss. That was quite a feature, as I recall. Not always, though.'

'And it's fatal?'

'Yes, that's to say it usually was then, or extremely nasty, but don't forget I'm talking about nearly forty years ago. It's only because of this doctor friend of mine that so many details have stuck in my mind. I'm sorry, Tim; I should probably have kept my mouth shut. After all, it was a foreign disease and, now I come to think about it, I only heard of it in a comparatively restricted locality, so why should it crop up here?'

'I don't know,' Tim answered wretchedly. 'But wouldn't that account for a man as experienced as Mr Cruikshank not recognizing it? And with all the mobility of population these days . . . Of course there's the six months' quarantine for animals from abroad.'

'I doubt if that would help over Primmer's disease. According to my friend the incubation period was completely elastic. The parasite could lie dormant for years or surface after a matter of days.'

'Oh, my God!' Tim frowned and sighed heavily. 'Well, all I can do now, I suppose, is try somehow to check up on the present incidence of the syndrome in this country – assuming there is one. Primmer's, you said?'

As the Colonel nodded, heaving Dreyfus upright, and made to leave, Tim wondered how much more he could take that day.

Yet worse was to follow. As he saw his old friend out they came face to face with Marjorie, the surgery cleaner, obviously admitted by Angela as she left. Her expression, a blend of guilt, accusation and sheer terror, plus the still disorderly state of the waiting-room, sufficed to tell him that she had managed to listen to almost every word of their conversation.

And not for nothing was she known in certain local circles as 'Marjorie Megamouth'.

5

Philip Anstruther, the newest vet in a small Oxford partnership, did rather wish he could be spared these pupils, assistants, lookers-on or however one cared to designate them. At any rate they came, one at a time, from a nearby girls' school as part of a project to determine their vocations careerwise. He wasn't very good with adolescent girls, at least not in his own estimation, and found them inhibiting to a degree.

There had been Anthea, stolid, silent, slightly baleful and a hundred per cent unresponsive to everything. Then Isabel, giggly and cheerful but with a positive flair for fading out of the picture when gruesomeness of any kind seemed to impend. Now he had Bernadette, the first one he couldn't help rather liking, yet in her way she was the worst of the lot, being over-addicted to philosophy.

'The Pope,' she announced suddenly, just as he was probing a particularly tender spot on a large Alsatian, 'has decided that animals have souls.'

'Really?' Philip reached for a pair of tweezers. 'How kind! *Ex cathedra* or merely *en passant*?'

That was a bit much for Bernie.

'Well, I mean to say, they have livers and kidneys and spleens and so on – just like us. So why not souls?'

'Why not indeed?' A warning growl from the Alsatian brought Philip's excavations to a temporary halt. 'If I remember aright, the anti-soul argument depends partly on animals being unable to make moral judgments.'

'So what?' Bernie was highly indignant. 'Moral judgments

or not, a lot of animals are a whole lot nicer than a lot of humans. Shouldn't niceness have anything to do with it?'

'Yes, well, I reckon so.'

Philip was rather relieved to be told that he was wanted on the telephone. Leaving Bernie and the Alsatian in the care of the veterinary nurse, he headed for the inner sanctum.

Tim Proud was just about the last person he expected to hear, diplomatic relations between them having once been at an all-time low due to a fierce and prolonged rivalry over a girl in their final year at college. He wasn't to know that he was the twelfth person Tim had contacted, so far unsuccessfully, over the old student network, but as they spoke they were both slightly surprised to find that all rancour had evaporated along with their youthful passion. The eleven practice runs had made Tim fluent and concise in what he had to say.

'So,' he ended after what of necessity had to be quite a recital, 'have you ever come across a case like this?'

'Can't say I have,' was Philip's unsurprising response. 'And I must say I hope I never do. So even your Mr Cruikshank can throw no light upon it?'

'Not a glimmer. But,' Tim added after a moment's hesitation before plunging, 'there's an old retired colonel here I've known for years. A very reliable type, down-to-earth, you know. Well, a bit weakly I suppose, I unburdened myself to him about it, and he seemed to recognize all the symptoms at once. Said it sounded like a parasitic thing called Primmer's disease that used to crop up in the Sudan years ago. Have you ever heard of Primmer's disease?'

Philip was quite definite that he had not.

'I must look it up.'

'I already have,' Tim told him. 'And everything the Colonel said about it fits. But what isn't right is that it shouldn't be happening in Britain, not unless some human or animal brought it in from abroad and passed it on through body fluids. Which is why I wondered if you had ever come across it.'

'No, I've no personal experience of anything like that, but what you said about the recurring symmetrical sores does seem to ring some kind of bell. I'm pretty sure it was a dog from round these parts, but as I never saw it myself I can't dredge up any details for you from memory. I'd have to talk to the other two vets in this practice. I can't remember which one of them it was; in fact it could even have been some report from before my time here.'

And likely enough at that, thought Tim, if the case had caused anything like the stress and upset poor Fritz Miller, as he now found himself thinking of him, was currently inflicting upon the Cruikshank establishment.

'Well, I tell you what,' said Philip quite amiably. 'Give me your home number as well as the surgery one and I'll do my best to find out and then ring you. The home one might be better, because then we can swap other news as well.'

'Definitely better,' Tim agreed wholeheartedly and did so. 'Thanks, Phil,' he ended and rang off.

6

Dr Alec Graylaw, the longest established and probably the most highly respected of the Somerstrand GPs, could hardly have felt less enthusiastic about his morning surgery that late spring day.

For one thing, altogether too much of the previous night's rain, assisted by a high wind in blocking a gutter with sodden and unseasonably dislodged leaves, had delivered itself down the back of his neck in a chilly cascade as he wrestled with the rusting lock of his up-and-over garage door. For another, the Prescotts, as always, had stayed on quite indecently late after dinner, and irritation about that, combined with Jill's over-rich salmon mousse, had done nothing for his digestion.

As he walked in through his waiting-room he assessed with a practised eye the small group of patients sitting expectantly on their wooden chairs. Most of them were well-known to him and unlikely to be suffering from anything too alarming. Or so he thought until his receptionist from behind her hatch cast him the strongest of her whole range of eloquent warning glances – Force Ten was how he liked to describe it – causing him another internal twinge and a slight, firmly suppressed belch.

Ellen Proctor, mother of Matthew, was the first to be called in. The finger she showed him was badly infected.

'I cut it trying to fix a hinge,' she explained apologetically. 'I did disinfect it, but it didn't seem to help.'

'All right,' he said, refraining from commenting that the fixing of hinges was generally more the husband's domain than the wife's. 'I'll give you an antibiotic for that and an antitet as well, just to be safe. What I'd like to know, though, is how you came by that nasty bruise on your cheek.'

The most transparently open of creatures, Ellen looked pathetically guilty. 'I'd forgotten to shut the door of the garden shed, and somehow I managed to walk into it in the dark. Not concentrating, I suppose. Stupid of me.'

'Oh yes? And you were blind drunk at the time presumably?'

He knew that she never touched alcohol. So, having given her the antitetanus jab and written out her prescription for the antibiotic, he leant back in his chair and forced himself to make the extra effort.

'Now come on, Ellen.' He'd known her long enough to see her through all the usual childhood infections, not to mention the little matter of Matthew's birth. 'What's going on all of a sudden in that house of yours? And not all that much of a sudden, come to that. It's Walter, isn't it? There's something wrong.' Something more wrong than usual, he omitted to say. 'Now there's no need to cry. We'll sort it. Just tell me.'

'I mustn't waste your time.' She fumbled in her pocket for a handkerchief. 'I can see how busy you are.'

'Never mind that. I know that lot out there. A few minutes' wait won't harm them. So let's have it. Walter hit you, didn't he?'

She nodded.

'I'm afraid so.' Plainly the confession was causing her some distress. 'I can still hardly believe it. I mean, he's never been the easiest person to live with, and I suppose we've gradually grown apart a bit, separate rooms and so forth, But in the past he'd never have done anything like that.'

'I should hope not!' Graylaw fished rather desperately in his drawer for a packet of Rennies he always kept there. 'Just a touch of indigestion,' he apologized. 'Sorry. Go on, Ellen. It doesn't mean I'm not listening. What's come over him, do you think? How long has this kind of thing been going on?'

She puckered her brow.

'Four or five months, I suppose. One minute he's his

normal self, the next he's flown into a terrible rage over some silly little triviality. I don't know whether he's worrying about something he won't tell me, but I've heard him being sick in the bathroom from time to time and put it down to drinking too much the night before. He does that sometimes if anything worries him. Another thing that makes me think he must be brooding over some problem is that he's apt to stumble over shallow steps or raised surfaces and sometimes bumps into odd bits of furniture as if he were too distracted to look where he's going. I've suggested several times that he should come to you for a check-up, but he won't hear of it.' She paused for breath. 'It isn't good for Matthew either. I didn't want him to go to boarding school so young – after all, he's hardly over twelve – but Walter insisted, and now I'm beginning to think it was just as well.'

'M'm.' Graylaw tapped a pencil thoughtfully on his desk. 'Poor Ellen.' Her parents, he knew, had been far from enthusiastic about her marriage to Walter, but they could never have expected this. 'Well, naturally I can't say what's wrong simply from what you've told me, but I do heartily agree that he should be checked over and if he won't come to me I'll just have to go to him. He'll be in tonight, will he?'

'He should be; he's just back from one of his business trips. But if he realizes what I've told you he'll be wild.'

'Then I'll make sure that he doesn't. I'll just drop in, say about seven, to ask how you are feeling now, and see what I can winkle out of him. OK?'

'Very OK.' She did her best to smile. 'Thank you, Dr Graylaw. You're always so kind.'

As he followed her out to pick up the next patient's file, Graylaw experienced an extremely unpleasant, almost eerie sensation that had nothing to do with his digestion. No, his every instinct told him, it was the atmosphere in the waiting-room, now considerably more crowded than when he had arrived, the concentrated way everyone was staring at him, as though suddenly hushed in mid-babble, the pile of magazines lying undisturbed on the central table. Something was wrong, no doubt about that and no doubt either that all too soon he would discover what.

Meanwhile, 'Mrs Eliot?' he called hopefully. 'Oh, just a moment, please.' An imperious flap of his receptionist's hand had returned the next patient to her chair and he found himself being almost pushed back into his consulting-room.

'I must talk to you, Doctor,' said the formidable Miss Evans. 'Urgently. This can't go on. You'll have to do something. It's that Marjorie Henshaw, second in the queue now. She's been telling them all the most terrible tales, scaring them half out of their wits.'

'Oh?'

'Yes, she's saying that there's some dreadful infectious disease spreading like wildfire through the town. Fatal, of course, and you've never heard of such a collection of symptoms. You simply must stop her somehow or we'll have a riot on our hands. And I'm not exaggerating.'

She rarely did.

What next, thought Graylaw, reaching for the third Rennie of the day. That's all we need.

'Right, I'll do my best.' Followed by a very starchy Miss Evans, he went out into the arena.

'Well, well,' he said repressively, after a prolonged and admonitory stare at the little assembly. 'What's all this Miss Evans tells me about some terrifying mystery disease in Somerstrand?'

Behind him he could sense her approval of the suitable note of incredulity.

'Well?' he repeated, as nobody seemed inclined to reply.

'I think perhaps you'd better ask Mrs Henshaw.' Miss Evans nodded ominously at Marjorie. 'She seems to be the sole authority on the subject.'

There was a long, deliberately dramatic pause while Graylaw concentrated his gaze upon Marjorie, but she was made of too stern stuff to be put down so easily by psychological means. With a deep breath she too went into action.

'It's some awful infectious foreign disease that both people and animals get. Kills you, it does. It's hard to pin down because at times it looks like all sorts of other illnesses and that's why they can't do nothing about it till it's too late. I mean to say, if somebody goes to the doctor with diarrhoea, he treats 'em for diarrhoea, dunne? Same with rheumatics or vomiting or going bald or whatever. And all the time it's this foreign illness. Ivy Miller's dog's got it, for one.'

'Really?' It wasn't often that Alec Graylaw had felt so inadequate. 'But who told you about this? Ivy, I presume?'

'No, she dun even know it herself yet. Which means that that dog of hers is going on spreading it right through the population. And so might she be, for all we know. She looks all right, but who's to tell? Might be festering inside of her all the time.'

'But Mrs Henshaw, if Ivy herself doesn't know, how can you?'

That was a bit of a facer, even for Marjorie, who shrugged defensively.

'I heard it when I was cleaning Mr Cruikshank's surgery. Colonel Power was discussing it with Mr Proud and even though the door was shut I heard it all, they talked so loudly.'

That was Graylaw's third really bad moment. In spite of his advanced age Colonel Power was still one of the soundest, most sensible people he had ever known and, worse still, he knew quite well that in spite of her failings, the gossip that Marjorie delighted in spreading usually turned out to be reasonably accurate. He resolved to see Tim at the first possible moment, but meanwhile she had somehow to be restrained.

'Well now,' he said with as much severity as his latest and imminent belch would permit, 'I know both the Colonel and Mr Proud well, and I've never thought of either of them as loud talkers. Yet you say that you weren't in the room with them, so all I can conclude is that you were eavesdropping – not a nice thing, would you say? And in view of the fact that according to you the door was closed, my guess is that you've got it all wrong. Now, if Mrs Eliot doesn't mind, I think it might be best if I saw you next before you upset anyone else any more. So what seems to be the trouble? Vomiting? Rheumatism? Thinning hair?'

He couldn't remember ever having been quite so rude to a patient.

7

Up in Middlemoor Clare Forrester was really going through it. For one thing, Rodrigo's condition had deteriorated to the point where he could no longer go to Alison as a day-dog. Instead Clare had to leave him alone in the flat, driving the two miles from work and back in her lunch hour to take him out and see that he was at least as all right as could be hoped. It was a fairly gruelling performance, in no way alleviated by constant evening visits to the vet, who was still as far as ever from making a diagnosis. The one person who came nearest to it was a grumpy old emergency stand-in twenty miles away whom she was obliged to visit one Sunday.

'I don't know exactly what it is,' he said testily, 'but I'm sure it's something parasitic and I wouldn't think the prognosis is at all good.' And went on, scowling, to imply that the whole situation was due to negligence on her part.

Nor were things at work at all cheering. After leaving Spain it had taken her several weeks to find her first job in Britain. Middlemoor was a good deal further from home than she would have chosen, but at least she was happy with the work itself and even more so that she had so soon met Paul Eddison, a kindred spirit who was doing rather well in landscape gardening and whom she now often saw. For well over a year now she had been employed by Robert Charters, an elderly, rather unassuming man who made full use of her Spanish and secretarial ability to promote his business of importing Spanish leather goods – shoes, belts, wallets, handbags and so forth, which were eventually distributed to UK retailers. She had also worked closely with Charters's manager, a much younger man, congenial and easy to get on with.

The rot began when he left to better himself and was succeeded by Gerald Barnet, who spelt trouble right from the start.

'He's rather dishy, isn't he?' enthused Sybil, the eighteen-year-old office-girl.

'Is he?' Clare responded. 'It hadn't struck me, but I'm sure he'd agree with you.'

'Well, I think he's quite interested in you, anyway. He's always peering over your shoulder.'

There she was right, but Clare was already fully aware that the interest was not personal, not in any flattering sense. She was soon to realize that he disliked her use of Catalan in the firm's considerable correspondence with producers in the Barcelona region.

'What's this?' he demanded one morning. 'The language, I mean.'

'Oh, Catalan,' she told him. 'What they speak in Catalonia.'

'Then how do you come to know it? It's not standard Spanish.'

'I lived near Barcelona for over four years.'

'But can't these manufacturers speak or write Spanish?'

'I'm sure they can; they'd have to. It's just that they're mostly very nationalistic in that they don't like being part of Spain and they love it when one uses their regional language. I'm pretty certain we get preferential treatment because of it.'

'Ah.'

He went out leaving Clare wondering uneasily what lay behind that little exchange. It took Anna, the typist from the outer office, to enlighten her.

'He has a girlfriend who speaks Spanish. I've heard him talking about it to her on the telephone.'

'I see,' Clare murmured. 'But not Catalan presumably.'

'All the same, there's really nothing he can do to get me out, is there?' she said to Paul one evening over a somewhat scratch supper in her flat; it was difficult for either of them to work up much of an appetite with Rodrigo lying on the hearthrug in such an apathetic state.

'Not unless he's an out-and-out sod,' he answered, 'though admittedly there are some about. But there's no point in worrying about it. Your job's the least of our headaches just now.'

Not long afterwards came the affair of the missing letter. It was a reply to a firm in Manresa which Clare well knew she had left on Charters's desk after finding him out of the office. A couple of days later he summoned her to complain that she had failed to write it.

'But I did,' she protested. 'I left it on your blotter. You were out. Sybil told me later that you'd gone to the bank.'

Just a little too hastily Barnet, hovering beside him, cut in with a great show of concern.

'No doubt you wrote it, Miss Forrester, but do you think you actually brought it here?'

'No,' she retorted angrily. 'I don't think. I know.'

'All the same, it might just be worth while having another look amongst your papers.'

Which she did and, predictably, found it, cunningly concealed inside an unaddressed envelope. As Paul said, there were certainly some sods about.

It took the vets concerned at the Middlemoor Veterinary Hospital, to which Rodrigo was finally admitted, a good deal of research, an assortment of tests and several days to diagnose his trouble.

'It's a parasitic thing called Primmer's disease,' Professor Bolsover, who was in charge of the case, told Clare. 'A tropical one that can only occur here if it is carried by a human or animal from somewhere in Africa, where it does crop up in small pockets. But you tell me Rodrigo comes from Spain?'

Trying to control her distress, Clare nodded. 'Yes, I got him from the *Protectora* in Barcelona when he was only a couple of months old. I did ask how he had come to be there, but all they could tell me was that some man had brought him along in a sack with a couple of other pups.'

'It's very strange.' Bolsover shook his shaggy grey head. 'Of course there's a lot of canine leishmaniasis in Spain. That's parasitic too and not dissimilar, but Primmer's has several quite distinctive features. Still, Barcelona's a busy port. Rodrigo's mother, or even grandmother, could have brought it in from Africa and handed it down to him through body fluids. Yes, that's by no means impossible. It's just a pity that we shall never know.' He broke off to look reflectively at her. 'It wouldn't be a bad thing if you were to have a blood test, by the way. Just as a precaution. Your doctor will advise you about that.'

'Oh, yes.' Clare was beginning to find it difficult to think straight. 'This other disease, the one you say is prevalent in Spain?'

'Canine leishmaniasis?'

'Yes. I've never heard of it and I've never met a dog with it.' Yet maybe she had, it occurred suddenly to her. An English couple she had known slightly, living near Barcelona, had owned two brought out from home and they both had been said to be suffering from some unpleasant and eventually fatal condition.

'How do the Spanish manage then, do you think?' she asked. 'Wouldn't you expect them to be scared?'

He shrugged.

'Well, it's up to them whether or not they keep dogs. If they do and it does happen, they have to choose between treatment and euthanasia. To be honest with you, I'd say that euthanasia is the more socially responsible course, as one dog can infect another, but they do have drugs out there - expensive, mind you - which can considerably delay the inevitable, particularly if the diagnosis is made in time. That's why humans with it have so much better a chance and often recover completely,' he added, plainly intending to allay any fears she might have on her own account. 'They can speak and complain of feeling ill long before the disease begins to show in the way it has to do in the case of an animal.'

'I see.' He was really quite a kind man, she registered vaguely. 'These drugs you mention. If the two diseases have similarities, would they be any help to Rodrigo?'

'They might be.' A gentle shrug suggested that the professor was not over-optimistic. 'We don't have them in this country, but we just might be able to get hold of some by means of a special import licence. The trouble is that it would take time and that, I fear, is definitely not on our side. Still, I'll have a try and see what we can do.'

And so shall I, thought Clare fiercely as, having bade Rodsey a rather heart-rending goodnight, she drove rapidly back to the flat to sift through the pile of documents he had caused her to amass.

It didn't take her long to find what she was seeking, the certificate of the antirabies vaccination he had been given on his arrival in Britain. He had had to be re-vaccinated, the Ministry of Agriculture, Fisheries and Food having been unprepared to accept the certificate for the one he had been given on departure. On the paper accompanying the British one was the address and telephone number of the veterinary practice that served the quarantine kennels where he had been. It was wildly unlikely that anyone there would be able to help over drugs, but anything was worth a try. They must surely come across the occasional dog from Africa.

A woman who sounded as if she were on the staff answered her call.

'How dreadful! How very distressing for you!' she exclaimed on hearing Clare's tale of woe. 'Mr Thompson will be sad too. No, we haven't any drugs like that, I'm afraid. I should think your only hope would be to contact somewhere where they specialize in tropical medicine. Now listen, dear, you won't touch him without wearing rubber gloves, will you? Some of these things can be very nasty, you know.'

Clare agreed that she did. 'But it's a bit late to worry about that now.'

'You haven't actually touched the sores? You did mention sores, didn't you?'

'Yes, I did. I have touched them the odd time, I suppose.'

'Then all I can advise you to do is see your doctor as soon as possible. He should know what to do. You will, won't you?'

'Yes, I will,' Clare lied, grateful in spite of her misery for such a show of concern.

She thanked the woman as warmly as she could and rang off.

8

No sooner had Alec Graylaw seen out the last of his patients, now with any luck at least temporarily subdued, than he hastened back into his consulting-room to dial Cruikshank's number.

'What on earth's going on with you, James?' he demanded when, after quite an interval, the receiver at the other end was lifted. 'And why are you answering your own telephone? It's Alec Graylaw,' he added, remembering that the elderly vet was not endowed with the best of ears for voice recognition.

'I'm answering my own telephone and cleaning my own disgusting surgery,' a furious voice informed him, 'in spite of having returned to work far too soon and being hardly able to walk, because Angela has an emergency dental appointment – or so she says – and that wretched young Proud's off somewhere messing around with a pregnant sow and, notwithstanding the fact that she should have put in a couple of hours here last evening, there's not been a sign nor a word from bloody Marjorie Henshaw all morning!'

'That's no surprise to me. She's been far too busy up here upsetting my other patients!'

'So what's wrong with her then, if your bloody Hippocratic oath will let you tell me? And when do you imagine I can expect her back?'

'I'd hate to predict. Very likely never, if she doesn't calm down. No, I reckon Marjorie's in pretty rude health. What I'd like to know is what's up with you and your patients?'

'My patients?'

'Yes, well, Ivy Miller's dog, to be more precise.'

'Ivy Miller's dog?' Cruikshank echoed after a pause in which shock evidently overcame excitability. 'What d'you know about that? And what the hell does Marjorie, come to that? And in any case, why should it be worrying her?'

As soothingly as possible Graylaw explained.

'This I find quite mind-boggling,' was Cruikshank's reaction after a long silence. 'Of course we've realized for some time that there's something very wrong with Ivy's dog, in fact I think young Proud was trying to make an appointment for it at Exleigh Veterinary Hospital. But as to Colonel Power and mysterious foreign diseases – that's going a bit over the top. Power's a sensible fellow, I've always thought. It's not like him to start scaremongering.'

'Exactly. And that's just why I'm worried. But even so we might have contained things if it hadn't been for Marjorie Henshaw. She's behaved appallingly, of course, eavesdropping and then spreading rumours all over the town. God knows where it will all end now. Mass hysteria if we don't play our cards right.'

'The only way we can hope to end it,' Cruikshank opined, 'is to get a reaction from the Veterinary Hospital as soon as they can or will produce one. I think I'd better ring them myself and put them in the picture. Anything to get things moving as soon as possible.'

Graylaw was in entire agreement.

'They're more likely to pay heed to you than to young Proud. There's just one thing, though,' he ended a little hesitantly. 'I'm chary of asking anyone else, but I suppose there's no way you could find out if the Miller dog was ever taken to the Proctors' house?'

'The Proctors' house? Oh, those people. Why should it have been?'

'Because Ivy Miller's their daily help.'

'Is she? If I ever knew, I'd forgotten. No, I very much doubt that. People don't usually take their dogs along when they go out charring. Why, you're not suggesting there's any tie-in there?'

'No.' Graylaw sounded doubtful. 'No, at least I hope not.

It's just that what Marjorie says bears a rather ominous resemblance to what Ellen Proctor told me about her Walter.'

When Tim Proud returned to the surgery after a fairly strenuous few hours in neighbouring villages it was to find Cruikshank angrily awaiting him, one leg stretched stiffly before him as he sat on a hard-backed chair.

'You've really done it this time, you young fool, blethering away to Colonel Power last night at the top of your voice!'

'Oh, that!' said Tim, recoiling. Mrs Cruikshank was a great believer in garlic perles, and not always of the odourless variety. 'I'd hoped you wouldn't hear anything about that, which is why I didn't bother you with it. Marjorie, I suppose?'

'Marjorie indeed!'

'So what precisely has she done?'

'Just put the wind up a gaggle of Graylaw's patients in his surgery this morning. He's extremely upset about it.'

'Oh Lord!' Tim groaned. 'That's all we need. The Colonel and I were talking perfectly normally – after all, neither of us is deaf – but I suppose the door's only chipboard and the wretched woman must have had her ear to the keyhole. I didn't even know she'd arrived until I almost knocked her over coming out. I did notice that she hadn't done any cleaning.'

'So did I!' said Cruikshank grimly.

'Well, it's not all negative, if that's any consolation to you.' Tim sighed. 'The Colonel gave me quite a lot of helpful information, including a possible name for whatever it is that's affecting Fritz, and this morning I made several enquiries amongst blokes who were in my year at vet school. One just might have something. Anyway he's going to ring me. And what's more, they've agreed to see Fritz at Exleigh tomorrow. I'll have to do something about transport.'

'Surely that's not your problem?'

'In this case I think it has to be. Poor old Ivy has had just about enough. Still, don't you worry. There's a lad in Clatworthy's garage I'm sure I can get to take them.'

That was when Sergeant Pearson elected to make his entrance, watched with fascination by the small group of pet owners who had arrived early for afternoon surgery in the hope of being first in the queue.

Safely closeted with Cruikshank and Tim, who went swiftly to join him, he announced, 'There's been a bit of a barney down at Tesco's. I thought perhaps you should know.'

'We should?' Suddenly remembering, Cruikshank lowered his voice almost to a whisper. 'A barney? What has that to do with us?'

'Well, it was between two women who I gather are associated with you, so to speak. A Mrs Henshaw and a Mrs Miller. Is that right?'

'In a sense, I suppose,' Tim agreed. 'So what happened?'

'Er . . . – well,' the sergeant seemed to be marshalling his explanations almost as if he were on the witness-stand, 'it seems that they met in one of the aisles there, and Mrs Henshaw was extremely offensive to Mrs Miller. Not foul language, strictly speaking, but bordering on it. Very insulting, at any rate. Mrs Henshaw accused Mrs Miller of being a threat to the whole town's health. Mrs Miller and also her dog. Does that convey anything to you?'

'To a certain extent,' Cruikshank answered cautiously.

'But to say that was totally unjustified,' put in Tim. 'Apart from being extremely unkind. The poor woman's going through it quite enough as it is, and she's probably going to lose her dog, who means a lot to her.'

'That's good,' said the sergeant with a certain smugness, until he caught Tim's eye and hastily added, 'well, in a manner of speaking, perhaps I should say. Anyway Mrs Miller hit Mrs Henshaw with a bottle of tonic water, plastic, fortunately, and the manager rang us at the station. So Constable Pringle and I went down there, but when we arrived the girls at the checkout refused to say anything except that whatever had happened to Mrs Henshaw she'd had coming to her, and if we'd any feelings we should take a look at Mrs Miller. And she did look a bit of a sight, I must admit. Very red-rimmed and so on.' At which point his descriptive abilities ran out.

'Oh dear,' said Tim. 'So what did you do?'

'Just cautioned them both, that's all. I couldn't see there was much harm done, except to Mrs Miller's feelings. Mrs Henshaw wasn't hurt.'

'Pity,' said Cruikshank. 'If I'd been there I'd have made it a glass bottle. Did anyone else see this performance?'

'Not many. A few shoppers, maybe half a dozen, and they just melted away without saying anything, if you understand.'

'Which doesn't mean that they won't be saying plenty later,' commented Tim after the sergeant had gone on his ponderous way. 'You know, I find all this very hard to take in at one go. I wonder if Ivy had any idea what was bugging Marjorie when she started in on her like that. If she hadn't, the shock must have been appalling. I don't think the sergeant said what time all this happened, did he?'

'No.' Cruikshank shook his head. 'Well, we'd better try to get through that lot out there before Ivy arrives up here with another bottle. And if she did you could hardly blame her. All this doesn't say much for our confidentiality.'

'Sorry,' Tim said penitently. 'I really am, you know. I wouldn't have had this happen for anything.'

Three dogs, two cats, one rabbit and a budgerigar later he and Cruikshank found themselves alone once more. As yet there had been no reaction from Ivy.

'I'll try to get down to see her before evening surgery,' Tim said. 'I owe her that at least. But what about Marjorie? What are we going to do about her?'

'Well, we certainly can't keep her, not after this. I've always known the woman was a potential menace, but this time she's overstepped the mark. If we show our disapproval by getting rid of her, it may at least counteract some of the damage she'll otherwise have done the practice.'

'With any luck she may dismiss herself,' Tim suggested hopefully. 'I mean, if she was so scared last night that she couldn't bring herself to clean up the place.'

'Oh, don't be idiotic!' Cruikshank snapped. 'That's just

what we don't want, implications that our surgery is some kind of death-dealing plague pit! No, we want to be the ones to do the dismissing, and be seen and known to have done it. For eavesdropping and spreading scurrilous, inaccurate and defamatory rumours through the town!'

'I suppose she's bound to realize that we know about that?'

'How could we not, after that bash up at Tesco? In a place the size of this? No, as I remember, Madame Marjorie must have a certain amount of pay due to her. And don't tell me she'll be too lily-livered to come up and collect that, if to do no more. And that,' he finished with almost sadistic relish, 'is when I shall scare the bloody pants off her!'

9

Tim's first port of call after leaving the surgery was Clatworthy's garage, on the landward edge of the town. There he found Jim Clatworthy in his office typing an invoice with a not over-clean finger while somehow managing to bark into his telephone at the same time. On seeing Tim he waved him to a chair and continued the altercation which, as far as Tim could judge, eventually ended in a draw. Just now almost everyone in Somerstrand seemed to be fighting over something, he thought glumly.

Fortunately, though, Jim was quite attached to Tim, whose parents had dealt with him over a long period, while in the last year or two Tim himself had managed to put a certain amount of business his way. Quite apart from having gone to a considerable amount of trouble over Jim's wife's ailing Yorkie.

'Hi, there!' Jim drew a deep breath in an effort to simmer down. 'What can I do for you, lad?'

'I've a bit of a problem over Ivy Miller, if her name means anything to you.'

Jim wrinkled his brow.

'Oh, aye, I know. Little fat woman from Jubilee Crescent.'

'That's right. Well, she and her dog need to be at Exleigh Veterinary Hospital by half past ten tomorrow morning. I'd take her myself if it weren't for the surgeries. It's a difficult case and I've a bad conscience about it, because my gut feeling tells me it's going to end in tears.'

'Oh. That's a pity. But anything that goes wrong won't be for lack of effort on your part, that I do know. Exleigh, you said. Two hours should do it. Say two and a half, just to be safe. Ben can take them. Will she be coming straight back, do you think?'

'That I don't know, unfortunately.' Tim looked more wretched than ever. 'It'll depend on what they say at the hospital. I'm afraid it will mean Ben having to hang around for a while, either way.'

'That doesn't matter; he's not all that busy just now. If she can pay for the petrol, I'll not charge her for anything else.'

'Thanks a lot, Jim, that's great of you.' Tim's spirits lifted slightly. 'I'll be glad to pay for the petrol; Ivy's forked out quite enough already and to very little purpose, I'm afraid. Now, if that's all right with you. How much?'

That left him time to get up to the school before Phoebe came out. On the pavement outside a group of mothers, some with prams, stood talking shrilly while waiting to collect their offspring. Something seemed to be exciting them and when they all turned to stare at him and his car he was left with little doubt what. Hastily he drove round the next corner, to linger until they had all dispersed.

Phoebe was still in her classroom, dealing with a pile of battered exercise books.

'Tim!' she exclaimed as she looked up. 'What on earth are you doing here? Has something happened?'

'You could say that. You won't have heard anything yet, but even without me it could only have been a matter of hours. Oh sorry, I've frightened you. It's nothing to be scared about in that way. Are you very busy just now, or will those books keep?'

'They'll keep. What is it? What do you want me to do?'

'Could you face coming down town with me and using a little diplomacy on Ivy Miller?'

'Ivy Miller? The woman with the dachshund?'

'That's right. I thought you said you knew her.'

'Yes, slightly, but that's all. I do know you've been very worried about the dog. So what's happened now?'

'Plenty.' Tim groaned. 'I'll tell you on the way. For

preference I'd like to get to her before her husband comes home. He's a great hulking brute of a fellow, as I remember, and he's not going to be at all pleased with me.'

They found Ivy sitting at her kitchen table, as had obviously been the neighbour who opened the door to them. In front of her was a large metal teapot with all the usual accessories, and by now she was looking what the sergeant would no doubt have described as very red-rimmed indeed. From his basket, in which he lay nearby, Fritz managed to agitate his whipcord tail very slightly in greeting to his medical adviser.

Ivy herself was a lot less welcoming.

'I don't know how you've got the gall to come round here, Mr Proud, I really don't. Not after all that's happened!'

'No, I must say I don't quite either,' Tim said gently, hoping that a soft answer would turn away her wrath. 'It took all the courage I could muster. You know Phoebe Fielding, don't you?'

'Hello, Mrs Miller,' Phoebe ventured with equal delicacy. 'You may remember me from school functions. I'm Tim's girlfriend, I suppose you could say.'

'Well, I suppose you could, seeing as everyone else does,' was Ivy's tart comeback.

'You must have had a terrible shock,' Phoebe pursued rather desperately. 'Mrs Henshaw has behaved appallingly. Tim says Mr Cruikshank wishes you'd hit her with something harder!'

'Huh!' Ivy snorted. 'Didn't want a prison sentence on top of everything else, did I?'

'Marjorie's not working for us after this,' Tim put in. 'We couldn't ever trust her again. What you won't know, of course, is that Angela let her in last night as she was going off duty, and I'd no idea she'd arrived – Marjorie, I mean. I usually let her in myself. Anyway, she must have put her ear to the keyhole of my closed consulting-room door and listened to an entire conversation I had with Colonel Power at the end of surgery.'

'Oh.' Digesting this, Ivy showed signs of becoming slightly mollified.

'I was discussing Fritz with the Colonel, you see, because he's a very old and respected friend, and this illness has been getting Mr Cruikshank and me down almost as much as it has you. Anyway, you'll be glad to hear that we've managed to make an appointment for Fritz at Exleigh. Tomorrow morning at half past ten. You can manage that, can't you? I know Mrs Proctor will understand.'

'Oh, I'm sure she will, but how do I get there?'

'Ben from Clatworthy's garage is going to drive you. There won't be any charge; I've fixed that. But he'll have to pick you up at eight o'clock. Will that be all right?'

'I reckon so. Ta. But what's this killer foreign disease Marjorie Henshaw was giving off about then? I don't see how my Fritz can have no foreign disease. He's never been abroad in all his life.'

'That's the sixty-four thousand dollar question,' Tim told her. 'The chances are that he hasn't at all. It was only that the Colonel was reminiscing about an illness he'd come up against in the Sudan years ago and it did seem to affect animals there in rather the way Fritz is beng affected. That's all. Just try to put it out of your mind until we know a bit more. We should pretty soon now.'

'M'm. So what's all this then about me being a source of infection and danger to the community? There's not often anything wrong with me that a couple of aspirins and a hot toddy can't put right.'

'Of course not,' Tim hastily reassured her. 'If that's what's being said it must just be some wild fantasy of Marjorie's.'

He had no intention of going into what the Colonel had said about humans, not if Marjorie hadn't already quoted it in the course of the Tesco fracas.

'Or something someone else has decided to tack on,' Phoebe added. 'You know what people can be like in a small town like this.'

No point, they had both decided simultaneously, in telling her of the morning's little drama at Dr Graylaw's surgery. Tim for one hoped to be as far away as possible when someone eventually did.

'Well, I just wish none of this had happened, apart from the appointment, that's to say. More tea, Sal?' Ivy waved the pot at her hovering neighbour. 'Sal's my friend,' she went on. 'It's things like this that show you who your real friends are. Do you know, this afternoon the woman next door rushed her blooming kids into the house when she saw me coming! And my sister-in-law usually drops in for a cuppa about now. But not a sight of hide nor hair of her today!'

'I'm so very sorry, Mrs Miller,' Phoebe said. 'You've been having a quite tough enough time without this to top everything.'

'I don't like hitting people in supermarkets.' Now Ivy sounded rather pathetic. 'It's not like me to get into quite such a rage. But when that woman said those dreadful things to me, right out of the blue, I felt like bursting, I did. I thought my head would split.'

'But have you ever had quite so much cause?' asked Phoebe, unaware of the sudden, almost electrical lurch of Tim's heart. 'Can't you have your evening meal fairly soon and go to bed early? Tomorrow's going to be a long and tiring day for you.'

The older woman nodded.

'Yes, I must be thinking about getting the tea. My hubby's working over at Windshot, but he should be home any time now. He'll get a shock when he hears about all this and just wait till he sees that Marjorie! She won't know if she's coming or going! They left in a bit of a hurry, didn't they?' she remarked to Sal as Tim propelled Phoebe with almost indecent haste out of the front door.

'You needn't have got quite so rattled about him, surely?' she protested as they drove off. 'Poor Ivy. She's very miserable, but I think you're pretty well forgiven.'

'Lord, I hope so. The trouble is, something tells me we're nowhere near the end of this affair. I could kick myself and strangle Marjorie.' He glanced at his watch. 'Evening surgery starts in half an hour. I'll just run you up to the school to collect your car.'

'Thanks. So see you later?'

'Of course, but would you mind very much if we had supper at my place instead of going out? Because I'm rather hoping for a telephone call from a bloke who was in my year. I rang him this morning amongst a lot of others to see if anyone else had come across a case of Primmer's disease in this country and he promised to dig out anything he could. Actually he was the only one who seemed to have a clue.'

'Well, that sounds quite hopeful. All right, I'll bring round the ingredients for a scratch supper. You look all in.'

'Wonderful,' he said as, reaching the school, he leant across to let her out. 'I'll ring you as soon as I get home. Could be a bit later than usual, what with all this drama. You were a great help with Ivy, by the way. I doubt if I could have calmed her down on my own.'

With a quick hug and a wave he was off again down the hill.

10

Back in her flat on the first floor of a tall Victorian house on the seafront, Phoebe hastily assembled the ingredients for a cheese and mushroom omelette, peeled and parboiled a few potatoes which could be finished off when she reached Tim, and added an apple pie, recently bought from the nearest bakery, plus a carton of long-life cream.

That done, she resumed work on the pile of books that she had retrieved from the school when she collected her car.

She was barely six from the bottom when her doorbell rang. What now, she wondered, and stuck her head out of the window. There below stood Mrs Bloomfield, gnawing her bottom lip and looking agitated.

'Mrs Bloomfield?' Phoebe called down to her. 'Just coming. Shan't be a second.'

It was the first time the headmistress had called unannounced, which almost certainly boded some kind of ill. But not at any rate in anti-Phoebe form.

'Is it all right if I come in for a moment, dear? I don't want to disturb you if you're busy.'

'Of course it's all right. Come on up, and I'll make us some tea.'

The few manoeuvres this involved allowed Mrs Bloomfield a brief interval to compose herself.

'I've just had a very peculiar telephone call from Mrs Hobbs,' she began, accepting a cup and the milk jug Phoebe pushed across to her.

'Carol's mother? But wouldn't any form of communication from her have to be peculiar? What's she complaining about this time?'

Mrs Bloomfield wriggled her shoulders in a helpless gesture.

'She's got hold of some quite extraordinary tale about a lethal infectious disease that's being spread around the town by some unfortunate woman and her dog.'

'Oh that,' said Phoebe. 'How did she come to hear that?'

'There was some kind of very unpleasant scene in Tesco's earlier today. Her sister was in there at the time and told her all about it. Now she's worrying about whether it's safe to let Carol come to school.' She peered sharply at Phoebe. 'You've heard something, haven't you? There's something in it, isn't there?'

'Honestly I don't know.' Phoebe passed her a chocolate finger. 'Tim's given me a resumé of what's happened, but I can't believe there's all that much reason to be scared. I'd be very scared on the dog's account if he were mine, but I don't think I'd go further than that. In any case, why should the school be more of a source of infection than any other public place, the shops or so forth? It isn't a question of measles or chickenpox or that kind of thing. I bet she was just fishing for information. So what did you say?'

'That I hadn't the slightest idea what she was talking about – which was absolutely true – and if she were worried all I could advise her to do was consult her family doctor, because if there were anything to know he'd be more likely to know it than I.'

Specially if he were Dr Graylaw, thought Phoebe, suppressing an unworthy grin.

'But the thing is, Phoebe,' Mrs Bloomfield leant forward earnestly, 'you are our weak link, don't you see? Mr Cruikshank's veterinary practice is the only one in Somerstrand' – touch wood, thought Phoebe – 'and everybody knows you are as good as engaged to Mr Proud. So obviously you are going to be bombarded with questions and you in a way will be representing the school.'

Definitely over the top, thought Phoebe.

'Oh, I'll be very careful. I don't see why I shouldn't tell you what I've heard, particularly as half the town already seems to be in on it, but no way am I taking it upon myself to answer anyone else's questions. I may be Tim's near-fiancée, but I'm certainly not his mouthpiece and Mr Cruikshank is already gunning for him over this. Not that it's in any way his fault.'

'Oh dear, dear, dear!' said Mrs Bloomfield at the end of what was an extremely brief account. 'What a really amazing business! So at least it has nothing to do with rabies? I'm sure that's the first thing that would occur to a lot of parents.'

'Heavens no, absolutely no question of that. If it had been, the dog would have died months ago. Please don't worry, Mrs Bloomfield. I'm sure it will all blow over in a few days. More tea?'

Tim's telephone call, when it came, was a good forty minutes later than usual which, in view of the headmistress's visit, made things easier for Phoebe. He seemed in better spirits when she arrived, and appreciative of the contents of her basket.

'I just wish you'd been there!' he exclaimed, bringing out beer-mugs. 'You'd have loved it. Talk about confrontation. Greek meeting Greek, you might say.'

'The Greeks being?'

'The Crook and Marjorie Megamouth!'

'So what happened? Thanks.' Phoebe took a deep swallow. 'Tell me.'

'Well, the Crook, Angela and I were there when she arrived. The last patient was just leaving. I did think old Marjorie looked fractionally nervous, but with a bit of bravado as well, and she took off her coat and went to the cupboard for her bucket and mop, and was just about to start work as usual when the Crook let her have it.'

'What did he say?'

'Oh, I can't remember exactly, but something to the effect of,' he struck a remarkably Cruikshank-like attitude, '"I can hardly credit, Mrs Henshaw, that you imagine there is still work for you here after all the poisonous rumours you have been spreading around the town today." And "Perhaps it's as well for the sake of your ear that Mr Proud's door opens inwards and not outwards." And "You must be relieved that being cautioned doesn't amount to having actually acquired a police record." And a whole lot more along those lines. Really quite impressive. You should have seen Angela's expression, especially when the Crook told her to fetch out the Megamouth's final pay-packet in its little brown envelope!'

'So how did the Megamouth react?'

'I must confess she gave just about as good as she got. She'd have done better not to fetch out her mop until she saw the way the wind was blowing, but she retrieved her position a bit by saying that nothing would have induced her to continue working beyond the end of the week on such contaminated premises, and for people who were so ignorant that they had to call in the help of batty old retired colonels. And, though it was of course of no account to her, there was such a thing as wrongful dismissal.' He refilled their glasses. 'To which the Crook replied that Ivy Miller might feel there was such a thing as defamation of character. Personally I wouldn't say it was exactly that, but something like it and quite good enough for Marjorie. Oh yes, and rather a nice final touch, I thought, the Crook said that if Marjorie were anxious to find other work, he did happen to know that the vicar was looking for someone to clean the church and probably wouldn't mind taking her on as he hadn't got a confessional!'

'What a performance!' Phoebe commented, laughing. 'All the same, I do wonder how you'll manage over the cleaning now. I wouldn't think this is quite the time to start looking for a replacement.'

'No, we thought of that, and Angela says she doesn't mind having a go for a few weeks until the dust has settled. Her boyfriend's off somewhere on a course.'

That was the most cheerful part of the evening. They ate their meal, washed up and started a crossword puzzle, but without great success; it was a particularly difficult one, and Tim's concentration kept slipping. After a particularly long pause Phoebe picked up the newspaper from the table between them and put it aside, to his fairly evident relief.

'It's that telephone call you're worrying about, isn't it? Honestly I don't think you can count on your friend ringing tonight. After all, it was only this morning that you spoke to him.'

'I know, but he did realize how worried we were and it wasn't anything very complicated that I asked him, just whether he or anyone else in that practice had ever encountered symptoms like Fritz's.'

At a quarter past ten the telephone did ring. Tim leapt to answer it and tried hard not to let his disappointment come across when he recognized Colonel Power's familiar tones.

'Tim? I don't like disturbing you so late, but I've come to the conclusion that I owe it to you to warn you about something.'

'Hello, Colonel,' Tim responded. 'About Marjorie Henshaw, I take it?'

'So you've heard the rumours. She's that wretched cleaning woman of yours?'

'Was. Mr Cruikshank fired her this evening.'

'Oh dear. But very wise, I should say, in view of everything. Still, I couldn't be sorrier for having been the one to put the cat among the pigeons.'

'You didn't. I unburdened myself to you and you made some comments which could yet turn out to be very helpful. The whole thing was due to sheer bad luck, plus bloody Marjorie's fundamental dishonesty and sensationalism. How did you come to hear about it, by the way?'

'My sister-in-law telephoned me. It was her bridge club afternoon, and they were all talking about it there. One of them was in Dr Graylaw's surgery this morning, which is when Marjorie, if that's her name, spilt the beans. I'm afraid the whole town will soon be buzzing with it, if it isn't already.'

'I'm sure.' Tim sighed. 'Well, I'm desperately sorry for Ivy Miller – the dog's owner, if you remember – but as to the rest of it, so what? Did you hear about the fight in the supermarket?'

'No, I didn't. What was that?'

'Oh, bloody Marjorie went for Ivy – verbally – and Ivy hit her.'

'Good God! Hard?'

'Not as hard as she deserved, but probably hard enough for Ivy's long-term good. The manager sent for the police, you see, and they each got a caution.'

The shocked silence at the other end of the line reminded Tim that the Colonel was rather more than elderly and his blood pressure probably not a hundred per cent.

'Oh, don't worry,' he added. 'I shouldn't have told you that, especially at this time of night.'

'If you hadn't, somebody else would have done. Tomorrow anyway.'

That was unquestionable.

'Look, Colonel,' Tim said earnestly, 'you go to bed and try to put the whole thing out of your mind. Ivy and the dog have an appointment at the Exleigh Veterinary Hospital in the morning, so with luck it won't be too long before the whole thing is sorted out one way or the other. I'm not over optimistic for the dog, but as for the rest of it I'm pretty sure it will all turn out to have been a storm in a teacup.'

'You're a good lad, Tim,' said the Colonel rather gruffly. 'Well, for everyone's sake I just hope so.'

11

'I suppose we'd better put him out for a minute,' Ivy said to her husband as they finished their scarcely touched meal on the night of Tim and Phoebe's visit. 'Do you think he's up to it? He seems to be seeing all right.'

'Reckon he'll be happier let out than stuck indoors wanting to pee.' Ned glanced at the clock. 'It's not a bad night and you can leave the door open. Bit early though, surely? Scarcely half nine.'

'We've got to get up a bit early,' she answered mournfully. 'What's the matter?'

'Just thought I heard summat outside. Bird, maybe.'

'Bit late for a bird. Still, I suppose it could have been.'

Piling the dishes and limping slightly, Ivy carried them over to the sink.

When approached, Fritz was reluctant to rouse himself, but eventually permitted her to propel him gently out into the back garden, where she left him while she dealt with the washing-up and Ned pondered whether there was any point in switching on the television.

They were both startled by the crash of breaking glass, quite a lot of it, to judge from the volume of sound.

'What the . . ?'

He dashed out in time to see a pair of hands release their grip on the top of the brick wall as their owner dropped back into the lane behind and bolted towards the main road, not alone, he judged, from the number of footfalls he could hear in the still air.

'Fritz! Is he all right?' Ivy shrieked as she hurried outside, still clutching a teatowel.

He was – relatively speaking – squatting in the corner nearest the house as if unaware of any disturbance.

'But the greenhouse isn't. Just look at that!'

What must have been quite a volley of stones, now lying in and alongside it, had smashed half a dozen of the panes. Inside several broken plant-pots had spewed their contents over Ned's tidy painted shelves. Further away and nearer to Fritz lay a solitary milk bottle, badly cracked but still recognizable as such.

'I'll ring the police,' said Ned abruptly. 'No good trying to chase that lot. Better bring Fritz in, though, just in case they come back.'

'But do we want to bring the police into it?'

'Why not? That's what they're there for.'

'Because of what happened in the supermarket. They weren't any too pleased with me.'

''Tweren't your fault. You didn't start it. And if there's any connection, all the more reason to phone them.'

Before the police could arrive the front doorbell rang.

'Who's that?' Ned demanded fiercely.

'It's only Sal. Are you all right? Can I come in?'

Passing the lane at the back of Jubilee Crescent on their way home from the pub, she and her husband had encountered a group of teenage boys, four of them, they were agreed, who had obviously been up to no good and had jeered and hooted at the Morrisons as they ran past.

'Jim couldn't take them on,' she said apologetically. 'Wouldn't have stood a chance, not at his age. But we did wonder if they'd been having a go at you.'

'Aye, they had,' Ned confirmed. 'Smashed the greenhouse, they did. We've rung the police. But what made you think it was more likely to be us than anyone else in the Crescent? You reckon it's to do with Fritz then?'

'Of course it's to do with Fritz!' his wife told him sharply. 'You wouldn't ask such a daft question if you'd seen the way some of the folks round here have been treating me since all this started. And why did they wait for me to put him out before they threw the stones? Probably hoped to hit him, poor little thing. Did you recognize any of them, Sal?'

'Yes, one of them was that lad of Maisie Cridland's. Right little tearaway he is, not to mention the gang he goes round with. I dursn't think what it'll be like when they get older.'

By the time Sergeant Pearson had arrived, inspected the damage, patted Ivy quite kindly on the shoulder and interrogated both Millers and Sal, any idea of an early night for Ned and Ivy was a thing of the past.

'The Lord help us,' she said desperately as she threw a clutch of cocoa cups into the washing-up bowl; in the sergeant's book partaking of cocoa did not qualify as drinking on duty. 'Statements all round at the police station tomorrow, when I've no idea when we'll be back from that vet place. And what will everyone say if I'm seen going in there? Which I will be, mark my words! Oh, goodness only knows where it will all end!'

This time her eyes really did overflow.

12

George Binding's peaceful slumbers were rudely interrupted in the small hours of that June morning by strident noises from below – the sounds of china being broken, glass splintered, kitchen utensils falling and, rising above everything, loud, furious caterwauling.

'Oh heavens, what now?' he groaned, heaving himself up into a sitting position.

'Invader!' his wife yelled up at him from already half way down the stairs. 'Must have come through the cat door. Orestes!' she shrieked, as she reached the now deserted kitchen and flung open the back door. 'Where are you? Come back.'

In a nearby house a bedroom light went on and in another somebody opened an upstairs window.

'Priscilla!' Still drowsy, George went stumbling after her as the sounds of feline strife died away in the distance. 'Please don't go after him, not dressed like that. It won't do any good. He'll be back quite soon, you'll see.'

'I just hope so.' Closing the door, she pounced upon a tuft of hair lying on the mat. 'Look! It must have been a black cat. I wonder whose.'

He yawned and gave a shrug.

'Doesn't matter. Wherever it lives, it'll be back now that it knows where it can find food ad lib. We'll have to get one of those magnetic cat doors and make him wear a collar.'

Yawning again and rubbing his eyes, he was still too sleepy to grasp what had earned him that unusually warm glance from his wife.

'Well, maybe,' she demurred. 'I don't really like the idea of cat collars. He could strangle himself.'

With a marathon effort he managed to regain total alertness.

'Unlikely, with so few trees round here. But otherwise, quite apart from the annoyance to ourselves and the neighbours, there's a far greater risk of him getting run over, chasing off in a state like that.'

'M'm.' She nodded. 'You're probably right. I'll go to the pet shop in the morning.'

By half past eight, by which time both Bindings were dressed and about, there was still no sign of Orestes.

'I'd have thought he'd be back by now,' Priscilla fretted, after the last fruitless shriek from the back door. 'Oh dear, in some ways dogs are less of a worry.'

Eventually, by which time George had endured several pieces of badly burnt toast topped by cold and watery scrambled egg – Priscilla was normally very good at scrambled egg – Mr Merson from next door put his head over their dividing fence.

'If you're worried about Orestes, I can tell you where he is. At the back of our potting shed. And from the look of him I think you'd better be the one to get him out. I really don't fancy it.'

'Oh!' Relieved and distressed in equal proportions, Priscilla tore off her apron. 'Thank goodness! I'll come right now. But your potting shed – that's astonishing!'

'It is rather.' Merson spoke dryly. 'In my experience he prefers flower beds. Got any protection, have you? He doesn't look too happy.'

Huddled at the back of the shed, just visible behind a pile of seed boxes, Orestes was indeed not in the best of shape. With an ear badly torn and one swelling paw held off the ground, he miaowed pathetically as Priscilla cleared the immediate area of garden equipment and gladly allowed her to pick him up.

'Just look at that paw,' she said to the two men. 'It's poisoned. That black brute must have bitten him badly. He'll have to go to the vet. It's too late for the morning surgery now, but I'm pretty sure there's one at lunchtime.'

Mr Cruikshank's surgery was of an unusual design, having originally been a pavilion belonging to the Somerstrand Bowling Club. It had two entrances, both at the front, separated by the width of the waiting-room into which one of them led. This was the one used by the patients; the other opened onto an L-shaped stone passage running along the side of Tim's consulting-room and round the back of Cruikshank's.

As Tim arrived for the afternoon surgery he saw the senior vet, still limping slightly, going in through the front. After they had finished they planned to ring the veterinary hospital to find out if there were as yet any news of Fritz.

That was when Tim had a very unpleasant shock. Glancing right as he locked his car boot, he recognized an approaching figure – Priscilla Binding, cradling in her arms a large and dejected-looking ginger cat. The shock came when he looked left and sighted another – Ellen Proctor, one hand heavily bandaged, slowly leading along a badly limping standard poodle. That gave him about twenty seconds in which to prevent their meeting. Desperation fuelled his brain.

'Afternoon, Mrs Binding,' he greeted her, going closer. 'Dear, dear, what's happened to your cat? A fight, by the look of him. What a mess! Come along in, through the back and I'll see him at once.'

Seizing his key, he unlocked the door.

'Oh, but I mustn't queue-crash,' protested Priscilla, surprised. 'That isn't fair. People won't like it.'

'Never mind about that,' he reassured her heartily. 'That fellow of yours is plainly suffering. The sooner he gets cleaned up and has an injection the better. Come on!'

Still slightly bewildered, Priscilla obeyed.

'Oh,' said Tim, once they were safely in his consulting-room, 'I'll have to have his card. What's his name? Orestes, isn't it? Just a moment. I'll fetch it.' Darting into Angela's cubby-hole, from where she was already taking registrations, he flicked through the filing-cabinet and extracted the one he sought. 'I've got the Binding woman and her cat in there,' he muttered softly to her. 'And the Proctor dog is waiting to see someone. It'll have to be the Crook.'

'Strewth!' exclaimed Angela, dismayed. 'So what do we do? She mustn't see the cat!'

'Well, the Binding woman's going to have to come out this way to pay, so we'll have to work that while the dog is in with the Crook. Is there anyone ahead of Mrs Proctor?'

'M'm. A bull-terrier pup. I don't think I've seen it before.'

'Then it's probably only an immunization; should be quick. So I'll deal with the cat and if necessary play for time till the poodle's gone in. Then you knock on my door, and I'll know it's safe to let the Binding woman out.'

'OK,' Angela agreed. 'The best of British luck!'

Still nervous, he returned to Priscilla.

'Let's see,' he said, cautiously handling Orestes, who seemed too miserable to offer much resistance. 'Yes, the ear's quite badly torn. I'll just clean it.' That was when Orestes did utter a loud protest. 'And there's an abscess on that leg where he must have been bitten; cats always have such dirty teeth, you know. I'll give him an injection' – he did so, at the same time listening for sounds from the neighbouring room – 'and a short course of antibiotics. Twice a day, starting from tomorrow.'

Reaching for a bottle that stood on a nearby shelf, he counted out eight and put them into an envelope on which he wrote the relevant instructions.

'Oh, thank you,' said Priscilla, preparing to leave. 'I was so worried about him.'

Still no knock. Tim was forced to improvise.

'Surely you can't cope with getting out the money while you're holding him? Wouldn't you like me to lend you a cat carrier? You can drop it back here any time.'

'Oh, no, no; it's very kind of you, but I can manage. My purse is in my pocket, so Angela can get it out and help herself.

We have a cat carrier, but he hates going in it.'

'Ah yes.' By now Tim was really up against it. 'That fight,' he remarked. 'Any idea how it happened?'

'Oh yes.' She explained about the night's events. 'And of course once that starts it's liable to go on happening.'

'You haven't a magnetic cat door?'

'Not magnetic, no, but I think . . .'

Which was when Angela knocked.

'I think you should definitely get one. Well, goodbye, both of you. And no more fighting, Orestes.'

Whereupon Priscilla found herself being practically thrust out into the waiting-room.

'Quite extraordinary,' she said later to George. 'One minute I thought we were there for the afternoon and the next he couldn't get rid of us fast enough. Yet he's always seemed such a normal young man.'

When Tim next saw his superior, three-quarters of an hour later, Cruikshank was looking quite shaken.

'Is it your leg?' Tim asked him. 'Still troubling you?'

'No. At least it is a bit, of course, but that's not what's worrying me. It's that poodle of the Proctors. I don't like it at all.'

'Well, I know it was limping,' Tim was too attuned to the situation to be misled by any ambiguity, 'but that doesn't have to mean anything.'

'No, I grant you it doesn't, but it's worse than that. He's got a sore on the ear as well - only one ear, admittedly, but it's horribly like the ones on the Miller dog. And,' he continued, before Tim could think of a reply, 'to crown everything, that unfortunate Proctor girl told me that her husband had one too, not in the same place, but very similar in shape and size. And apparently he hasn't been at all well for some time. I really think I'll have to have a word with Graylaw.'

13

Clare was growing more and more to dread her evening visits to the veterinary hospital. Thanks to a helpful contact at the Liverpool School of Tropical Medicine, Professor Bolsover had actually managed to obtain a small quantity of a drug used abroad in the treatment of Primmer's disease, but he was still awaiting further supplies in his own right.

'We have to get an import licence from the Veterinary Medicines Directorate,' he explained pontifically to Clare, who had already grasped that and could hardly have cared less about further technicalities, 'under the Medicines Act of 1968.'

Meanwhile Rodrigo was showing no improvement.

'You know, this really isn't kind.' The older of the two veterinary nurses broke the long silence as she and Clare sat alone together in the near-twilight watching over him. 'Goodness knows I understand how you feel, but I think you're going to have to face the fact that it's too late to help him, and what's he getting out of life, going on like this? I know he perks up a bit when he sees you, but the moment you leave he's right down again.'

'But Professor Bolsover must think there's at least some chance,' Clare protested, almost hating her for coming out with what she already knew in her heart was the truth. 'Otherwise he wouldn't go on trying, would he?'

'Wouldn't he? I've no doubt he imagines we're learning something from all this misery – after all, how many cases like this will they ever have had to deal with here? I don't doubt that other animals will eventually benefit, but don't tell me Rodrigo will. Just ask yourself why he's charging you so comparatively little when the treatment has to be costing a bomb. Personally I don't think this kind of thing is fair.'

But she, Clare knew, having heard all about it during their several vigils, had just had to have her own dog put down and was suffering the after-effects. Sadly she looked at the little fox-terrier in the next cubicle. He, at least, was going to survive.

'Well, I'll see,' she said, stroking Rodrigo's head and rising to go. 'Maybe things will become clearer in a day or so,' and departed hastily before she disgraced herself by bursting into tears.

The following morning brought a glimmer of cheer to the office in the form of Salvador Torres, the traveller from Carrasco's, the Tarragona shoe manufacturers. Clare knew him quite well; he would look in to see Mr Charters every two or three months, bringing samples and details of new lines, and had helped entertain her and Bob Hastings, Barnet's predecessor, during the previous summer's trades fair in Barcelona. He had yet to meet Barnet.

Coming into Clare's little office, he greeted her warmly.

'I understand that Bob's been replaced. That's a pity. What's the new man like?'

'Awful.' She grimaced. 'I expect he'll be all right with you, but watch what you say. I wouldn't trust him as far as I could throw him!'

'But you'll be coming over with him to this year's trades fair?'

'I hope so, but I wouldn't count on it. I reckon he'll sabotage that if he can.'

At which point Anna's head came round the door.

'Sorry to keep you waiting, Señor Torres; they shouldn't be long. Coffee? I'm just making some.'

'Yes, please. That would be nice.' He sat down on the chair Clare pushed towards him. 'It's rather pleasant to be over here just now. Much cooler than with us. Well, what's your news, Clare? How's Paul? And how's my little compatriot these days?'

'Rodrigo? Well, I'm afraid that's a sad story.'

Briefly she explained.

Salvador was distressed.

'So that's why you're looking so peaky. What a tragedy after all you went through to get him back here. It's an awful thing, that disease.'

'Oh?' she queried. 'Surely you can't have come across it? They tell me it's something from Africa.'

'Africa? I shouldn't have thought so. Quite a lot of dogs in Spain go down with something that sounds very much like what you've described.'

'I think that will be canine leishmaniasis,' she told him, remembering what Bolsover had said. 'Apparently it isn't the same. Rather similar, admittedly.'

'But Rodrigo was born in Spain, wasn't he? And never left there until he came here?' Salvador looked incredulous.

'Yes, but . . .' Quickly she recounted Bolsover's theory regarding the potential hazards of ports like Barcelona.

'I suppose that's possible.' Salvador didn't seem entirely convinced. 'We do have quite a large Moroccan and Algerian population too, as well as people coming up from the extreme south. It could conceivably have happened through one of them.'

'Maybe,' she agreed. 'Anyway it's all pure theorizing, because it's something we can never know for sure.'

After a longish session with Charters and Barnet he looked in on her again to say goodbye.

'Well?' she demanded. 'Successful?'

'I think so. Much as usual, at any rate. But Mr Charters isn't looking too bright, is he? He seems to have aged since last I saw him and that's only a couple of months ago.'

'Yes, possibly he has. And Barnet? What did you make of him?'

Salvador switched on his rather attractive lopsided grin.

'It's hard to say on so short an acquaintance. Inclined to be a shade overdynamic, perhaps?'

'He's that all right.' She had to laugh at the description. 'Next time you come you'll probably find we've all aged!'

'No, you mustn't let him do that to you,' said Salvador quite kindly, with another somewhat penetrating look. He liked Clare. 'Find another job rather than that; with your qualifications it shouldn't be too difficult. But not before the trades fair. That isn't so far off now.'

Barnet himself appeared shortly afterwards, unfortunately catching her in the act of locking her drawer prior to going out to lunch. The hidden letter she had simply given to Charters, claiming that it was a copy of the original that had so mysteriously disappeared.

'Secrets?' Raising his brows, he looked uncommonly pleased with himself.

'Well, you know how things are.' She shrugged, putting on her jacket.

Barnet was quite unabashed.

'I just looked in to say that Mr Charters wants you to do some telephoning with him when you get back this afternoon. About two o'clock should do.'

'Three o'clock over there? Yes, that usually seems quite a good time.'

Salvador had been right, she thought later on, as she sat down beside Charters and prepared to do his interpreting. His complexion had taken on a faintly greyish tinge, and he did indeed look as if he had suddenly aged. Was Barnet's forcefulness and excessive energy in some way sapping his vitality, she wondered, or had he recently developed a health problem?

When they had finished the telephoning, a fairly wearying process involving much discussion about discounts and quantities suitable for Christmas, he took off his spectacles and turned to her.

'I'm sorry about your dog, my dear. Very distressing for you.'

'Salvador told you, did he?'

'Yes, he did. The circumstances seem so unusual and he evidently thinks quite a lot of you.'

'Um,' she responded, enbarrassed.

'So it occurred to me that when this has – er – resolved itself you might like to think about taking your holiday. Have you any plans?'

'Not as yet.'

'Well, in any case it couldn't be for the next two or three weeks, because as you know, the busiest time of the year is just coming up. But after that, perhaps?'

'But there's the trades fair. I was very much hoping to go to that again.'

'Ah yes.' Embarrassed in his turn, he fiddled with the papers in front of him. 'Well, as it happens I shan't be needing to send you this year. Barnet has no Spanish, of course, or very little, but by a happy chance his young lady is going to be over there at the time, staying with friends, and is apparently quite taken with the idea of interpreting for him. She won't know anything about the business side, of course, as you would have done, but he does, so I see no reason why they shouldn't work quite well together. She will have to be paid a small remuneration, but even so it will save us quite a lot of expense.'

Clare felt her face grow scarlet with a fury such as she had hardly ever experienced. Not because of the trades fair or Charters's evident manipulatability, but because Barnet had got away with it again.

Worse was to follow.

'One consolation, though. Till now I haven't been able to let you go for more than a fortnight at a time, but because of her you can have the whole month at one go if you like. She has her own job in the town, but she's told Barnet that if you were away she would be prepared to come in here the odd evening after work to do your letters and no doubt we could organize something about any telephoning necessary.'

'Oh, would she? Still, I don't think . . .'

'For which reason,' Charters continued, 'Barnet thinks it might be as well if you dropped the Catalan for the next few weeks and confined yourself to Castilian.'

Clare made a monumental effort at self-control.

'All right, if that's what you want. A lot of the suppliers won't like it, but if she can't manage Catalan that's all there is to it.'

No point in saying more. Leave she would undoubtedly have to, whether voluntarily or edged out by Barnet, but certainly not before the holiday nor without a reference from Charters.

She was still seething when she reached home, so much so that she managed to unlock her door without immediately noticing Paul's car parked outside.

'Paul!' she exclaimed, startled, when she did. 'What are you doing here at this time? Has something happened?' And, seeing his expression, 'Oh . . . But when? And how did you know?'

'I'm so very sorry, Clare. Come and sit in the car for a moment. I didn't tell you, but I rang the veterinary hospital a few days ago and asked them to give me a ring at work if it should happen. I didn't want you to have to go through this on your own. Here.'

He reached for a handkerchief.

'It's all right. I've got one.'

'This will be better. Bigger. It was this afternoon,' he went on. 'Very peacefully, they said. I know how you're going to feel, but at least we can be thankful that you didn't have to make the horrible decision yourself. Because that's what it would have come to in the end. They as good as admitted it. And I knew you wouldn't want them to deal with him, so I went down there to fetch him.'

'Oh, Paul.'

She could hardly speak for tears.

'He's under the rug in the back. We can bury him in my parents' garden tomorrow, perhaps. There's a pretty little corner in the rose bed.'

'You are a dear, dear thing,' she said. 'But I'll have to go down there myself to say goodbye and thank them.'

'I know. I told them you would, but not this evening. You've had enough for one day . . . The other thing,' he added much later when they were indoors, 'is that they said it would be as well if you went to the Infectious Diseases Hospital for a blood-test. It's quite lucky there's one here.'

'Yes, they've already told me that, but they weren't

particularly pressing about it.'

'Maybe not.' His expression was anxious. 'Even so, I'd get on with it if I were you. It will probably be quite all right, but they may not realize quite how closely you've lived with him, letting him come into your bed and so forth. Now you will, Clare, won't you? It would be sheer lunacy not to.'

'Yes, I will, but it can't be for another three weeks or so, not while the abysmal Barnet is around. We're just coming up to the busiest time of the year, as poor old Charters reminded me this afternoon.'

14

The morning after Tim's visit to Clatworthy's garage Ben duly collected Ivy for the Exleigh trip, holding Fritz while she settled herself and a carrier bag in the passenger seat and then placed him on her lap, where he flopped with obvious relief. Ivy was looking exhausted; the previous night's vandalism of the Miller greenhouse plus her distress over the dog had plainly taken their toll.

'Right then,' he said cheerfully, 'here we go! At any rate we've got a fine day for the drive.' Although they lived at opposite ends of the town, he knew her by sight and had tinkered with her husband's lorry from time to time. It was the first occasion, though, that he had noticed her awkward way of walking.

'Trouble with your leg?'

'Just a touch of arthritis. Or rheumatism, maybe.'

Dunster, the first village on their way, was crowded with visitors recently decanted from a couple of tourist buses, busily photographing the Yarn Market with its castle background or scrutinizing the postcards and souvenirs displayed outside the shops on either pavement. A sharp fork to the right, along a perilously narrow street leading past the church, a gentler one to the left which brought them to a rather wider and more residential road and they were away and out into the wilds.

He had been right about the day; rain had fallen during the night, leaving the countryside looking its best, sunbeams gleaming on the freshly washed leaves of the trees which stood thick alongside the twisting road or behind the high banks which appeared from time to time. At intervals their route took them across brief stretches of moorland, then passed through some upland village with scarcely a soul about.

A countryman at heart, Ben was happy to be away from the heat and fumes of the garage, and would have been happier still had he felt that Ivy was in any state to share his enjoyment.

'Doesn't look too good, do he?' he said, glancing sideways as they passed through Wheddon Cross. 'Still, you're taking him to the best place, I'm sure. What's the trouble, do you know?'

She shook her head.

'Not rightly, I don't, nor Mr Proud neither, but that don't stop half the folks in Somerstrand making up their own stories about it. You'll have heard things by now, I don't doubt.'

'All I've heard,' Ben came from a household dominated from across the road by two unmarried aunts and three cats, which had developed in him a certain flair for dealing with middle-aged females in distress, 'is that old Marge Henshaw started shooting off her mouth about something she'd heard, or thought she'd heard, at the vets' and that you coshed her in the supermarket. Fair made my mum and dad's evening, that did; they reckoned you deserved a medal. She's a right pain in the arse, is that Marge.'

'She's that all right.' The vestige of a smile briefly lit up Ivy's tear-blotched face. 'But hadn't you heard that Fritz and I are meant to be spreading some horrible disease through the town? Hadn't you heard that when you picked us up?'

'Oh that.' Slightly at a loss, Ben took one hand for a second off the wheel to scratch the back of his head. 'I think maybe Mum heard tell of that, not in any detail, though. But nobody in his right mind pays any heed to that kind of claptrap. People can get right peculiar when a lot of them together work themselves up into a tizzy. Strike sparks off each other, if you know what I mean. Not worth bothering oneself about.'

Ivy looked grim.

'Ned and I had to take notice all right last night when a gang of lads came into the garden and smashed our greenhouse.'

'No!' Ben was horrified. 'They never! Any idea who 'twas?'

'Maisie Cridland's son, for one, according to my friend Sal. She and her hubby saw them running out of our back lane.'

'Told the police, have you?'

'Yes, the sergeant came along last night, but that's not to say they'll be able to do anything.'

'Cor!' Ben shook his head in disbelief. 'Mindless little bleeders! A good walloping's what they need. Folks are too soft these days.'

He glared at the driver of an oncoming car which was taking up far more than its share of the road.

'One thing, though,' Ivy continued, 'I know who I won't be speaking to after all this is over, and that's just about half of Jubilee Terrace. The girls in the supermarket were nice, though,' she added reflectively. 'They stuck up for me when I hit that Marge Henshaw. Would you like a drink, lovey?' Fishing in her bag, she brought out a bottle of water and a dog bowl.

Exleigh Veterinary Hospital, which wasn't hard to find, stood imposingly on a hill on the outskirts of the town.

'I'll be here when you come out, no matter when,' said Ben. 'Just you try to take it easy, Mrs Miller, and the best of luck, old son.' Patting the semi-inert Fritz as he took him so as to enable Ivy to clamber out, he was hit by a wave of sadness. Poor old cow; people might get a kick out of their pets, but no way was it always all beer and skittles.

Once inside, Ivy found herself standing in a stone-flagged hall, clutching Fritz while waiting for a girl behind the reception desk to end what sounded like a social and fairly absorbing telephone call.

'Yes?' she said, when finally she did so. 'How can I help you?'

'I'm Mrs Miller,' Ivy answered, resentment welling up through her weariness. 'From Somerstrand. Mr Proud, the vet there, arranged for my dog to be seen by somebody here. He isn't at all well. The dog, I mean.'

'Oh,' said the girl with a little more show of concern, and rang the press-button bell beside her. 'Shan't keep you long.'

Moments later a white-overalled woman appeared.

'It's Mrs Miller from Somerstrand,' the girl explained. 'She's expected.'

'Oh yes. Good morning, Mrs Miller. I'll just take him, shall I? What's his name?'

'Fritz,' Ivy answered. 'But aren't I going to see nobody? Do I wait here or what?'

'Oh, but you can't take him home again this morning.' The woman looked quite taken aback. 'We'll need to keep him for a day or two at least. Didn't anyone warn you?'

'No, they didn't,' Ivy countered. 'Nobody told me nothing. I would like to see someone, though. I'm not going off home leaving him like this.'

Her opponent stared briefly, then capitulated, seeming to realize that the little fat woman had a point.

'All right; I'll ask Mr Brimson to come and have a word with you. He's rather busy just now, but I expect he will.'

She bustled off with Fritz, to return two or three minutes later accompanied by an elderly man with gold-rimmed spectacles and a greying tonsure.

'Mrs Miller?' he greeted her. 'You didn't realize that you'd have to leave your dog here with us? Isn't that all right?'

'I suppose so.' By now poor Ivy was near to tears. 'So long as I get him back. I will, won't I?'

Brimson wagged his head doubtfully.

'Well, I'm afraid I can't promise anything, Mrs Miller, only that he'll be in good hands and we'll do our very best for him. I've spoken to both Mr Cruikshank and Mr Proud about the case and it certainly isn't something we come across every day. All I can suggest is that you go home now and do your best not to worry. We'll contact Mr Proud the moment we know anything. Would you like one of the nurses to get you a cup of tea? You don't look any too well yourself.'

'No, ta very much,' said Ivy, blinking hard and drawing a deep breath. 'I'm just upset, that's all. So I'll be off then.'

In Somerstrand that evening Tim was again insisting on staying in.

'You don't mind, do you?' he asked Phoebe. 'Phil must surely ring tonight. And I've organized the supper.'

'No, I don't mind,' she agreed. 'Of course not. But do you have to be quite so tense about it now that someone more high-powered than you or the Crook is dealing with Ivy's dog?'

'No, I don't; that's true. Still, it would be nice to have a chat with Phil. There was a time when we were pretty good pals.'

Meanwhile Phoebe had her own experiences to recount.

'You know, I think we'd have a fit if we knew half the things that are being said about all this. I'm not worrying you, though, am I?'

'Oh no,' he said rather wildly. 'Feel free. Carry on.'

'Well, the woman in the sub-post office, the sour one with the horn-rimmed glasses who normally can hardly bother to speak to me, wanted to know how I was these days. And the man in the bakery and the chemist's assistant were a whole lot more forthcoming than usual. They were obviously hoping I'd tell them something.'

'And did you?'

'Of course not. Don't be stupid. But the *pièce de résistance* – this you'll scarcely credit – happened this morning. When I went into my classroom, rather early, as luck would have it, there were three little girls, ten-year-olds, all with their pants down, counting their own and each other's pubic hairs. None of them had any worth speaking about, naturally, but it was obviously a matter of deep concern.'

'Really? Well, it sounds a bit eccentric, but you know what kids are. Aren't most little girls rather intrigued when they sprout the odd one or two? I seem to remember that my sister was.'

'No, no, no, you're missing the point.' Phoebe was exasperated. 'It's Primmer's disease, don't you see? Hair loss. One of the symptoms as divulged by Marjorie Henshaw. And, if you don't believe me, I heard one of them say, "Well, my mum says my dad's always been bald and bad-tempered, so what's new about that?"'

'I think I need a drink,' said Tim. 'So what did you do? Tick them off? Send them to Mrs Bloomfield?'

'Oh, no. Fatal. She'd have had a heart attack. No, I just gasped in amazement – genuine enough, I can tell you – and told them that if anyone else heard what they'd been up to they'd be the laughing-stock of the whole school.'

'I hope they believed you. To think that all this is probably being laid at my door . . .'

'And the Colonel's. Listen. Telephone.'

She stopped short, her sharp ears having picked up the faint tinkle that preceded a proper ring. This time it really was Phil.

'Sorry I didn't get you last night,' he said. 'The thing was, it wasn't one of the blokes here now who was involved with a case of Primmer's disease. It was someone who'd left Oxford and since retired to Suffolk, so I had to track him down through the telephone directory. Anyway I finally got him and he said it must have been about ten years ago, and it was a dog from somewhere in Africa, and there really couldn't be any connection with your case, if that's what it really is. And he's never in his whole career heard of another in Britain and that's what the chaps here also say. Does that help?'

'Of course it does. In a negative kind of way, but even that's something. Thanks a lot, Phil.'

There followed a lengthy conversation about their shared past, things they had done together, people they had known and how they were faring at present. Half-listening from the kitchen, where she was putting the finishing touches to Tim's culinary efforts, Phoebe was glad that he was beginning to sound so much more relaxed. Then his tone changed.

'Oh, my God! Are you sure? That's a bit of a shaker. No, no, it may not matter; anyway I hope not. No point in going into that now – it's far too involved – but I'll tell you all when the dust has settled.'

'So what was all that about?' Hearing the receiver being replaced, Phoebe returned to the sitting room. 'The total change in your manner and the sudden "My God"-ing?'

Tim seized his glass and took a particularly deep swallow.

'One little detail that came back to Phil right at the end. Something the Colonel presumably can't have known about, thank Heaven, or by now Marjorie would have spread it all round the town.'

'What?'

'Cats. According to Phil, who got it from the contact in Suffolk, though cats never show any symptoms of the disease, they can carry it.'

'So? Oh, I see.' Her eyes widened. 'The Binding cat!'

'Who used to be the Proctor cat and would be a safely dead Proctor cat now if it hadn't been for me. Exactly. So what do I do now? If this ever gets out, I'll be in it up to the eyeballs, yet he'll have to have a blood test. Somehow.'

'But don't you think you can take a chance on it? Surely he isn't very likely to be a carrier?'

'Well, admittedly there's nothing definite as yet, but the Crook reckons that the Proctor poodle must have it, not to mention old Proctor himself. Because of those weird sores, you see. And the cat must have spent his first year or so in that household. No, just think, Phoebe. What if sooner or later one or both of the Bindings developed it? Apart from the horrible effect on them, everyone would be completely mystified, not to say panic-stricken, and only you, Angela and I would know the truth. No, I've got to think of something.'

'Why don't you tell Mrs Binding the whole story and ask her to let you do the test? I don't see how she can really blame you. You said at the time there was no possibility of your finding him another home and that if you'd refused to put him down yourself the Proctors would simply have taken him elsewhere. Surely any decent-thinking person would agree that it was right to give him a chance at least, a young, healthy cat like that?'

'I doubt if the Crook would see it that way. Don't forget that I took the fee for putting him down. Admittedly I had no alternative and I didn't get it myself – it went into the Crook's coffers – but even so . . . No, I'd really rather not tell the Binding woman if I can possibly avoid it. Don't forget that I was the one who started the whole furore. The cat affair on top of that would probably put paid to my whole career.'

'You'll have to tell her if the test is positive.'

'Oh yes, then, but with any luck it won't be. Sufficient unto the day!'

'All right.' Phoebe sighed. 'Let's think then. How do you do it? You can hardly lurk in the road and seize him when he comes out for an evening stroll! For one thing, you'd probably be seen.'

'That isn't funny.' Tim was cross. 'No, of course I can't. No, now wait a moment. He's just been in with an abscess and a damaged ear. What if I told her I thought I ought to see him again, just to be sure he's healed up properly?'

'But she'd bring him in and stay with him all the time. You couldn't take a blood sample without her noticing, could you?'

'Not a hope. I'd need at least three minutes alone with him. Still, with Angela's cooperation it just might be worked. We'd have to create some kind of diversion to distract Mrs Binding. It's just possible. I'll have to sleep on it.'

'Well, I think you're crazy.' It was Phoebe's turn to be cross. 'What have you been reading? *The Boys' Own Paper*? All I can say is that as soon as we've had our meal you'd better start sleeping and I'll be off home. Thank goodness it's nearly the end of term!'

15

Tim's sleeping on it proved in fact to be not sleeping on it. He had a rough night, plagued by an overactive mind, and by morning was tired, irritable and no nearer to finding an answer to the Orestes problem. Even so, he managed to get himself to the surgery before either Cruikshank or the first patients had arrived. As he had hoped, he found Angela already there, mopping the floor as Marjorie would normally have done the previous evening. She was shocked to hear of the latest development, or at least as shocked as her effervescent nature would allow, and entirely agreed that the cat must have a blood test as soon as possible.

'But as you'll presumably have to post the sample to Bristol, what's to stop the Crook opening the reply, if it comes by post too? Or taking a telephone call, come to that?'

Tim groaned.

'Nothing. Absolutely nothing. Oh, hell!'

'Now, don't be so defeatist,' Angela said briskly. 'Let's just think.' She pressed her dripping mop down on the perforated half-cover of a galvanised iron bucket. 'Yes, well how about sending them a letter with the sample? Not just the covering note, I mean. Say you're dealing with the case on your own, as the Crook is battling with a load of work and a badly hurt leg, and you don't want him to suffer any avoidable extra stress.'

Tim snorted.

'So you will ring them in a couple of days or so, and if that's too soon you'll just keep trying until they do know something. How about that?'

He pulled a face.

'Not brilliant, but quite as good as anything I could have thought of. Of course, if they're at all like my bank, it would be safer to ask them to make certain that the Crook alone gets the verdict.'

'That's being defeatist again,' Angela retorted. 'Surely no reputable medical establishment could be as inefficient as your bank. Now we'll have to arrange an appointment for Orestes at a time when nobody but you and me is around. No Crook, no patients.' She squeezed the mop again. 'But that could be difficult since Mrs B. isn't going to see any reason for fixing a definite time, not with three surgeries a day. Hadn't you better take a little time to work that one out rather than hurry and mess it up?'

'That's all very well,' he argued a shade querulously, 'but if we do it after he's had time to heal up it will look plumb ridiculous. It really should be within the next twenty-four hours or so.'

Yet twenty-four hours later they were no further.

Cruikshank was more than morose after lunch, when he had his first chance to talk to them in private.

'It's been a filthy morning,' he grumbled. 'I rang Graylaw last night – it would have been criminal not to let him know what Ellen Proctor told me about her husband's sores – and he rang me back after his morning surgery. He'd already visited Proctor because the girl was so worried about him and found him actually prepared to admit that he was in pretty bad shape. And coming from Proctor that was a lot, he said. It seems he usually prefers to take things out on his family rather than complain to a doctor on his own account. Anyway he's gone to hospital, not here, but the infectious diseases place at Bristol and the fellow there had told Graylaw that the prognosis is far from good.'

'I'm sorry,' said Tim. 'And it is the Colonel's Primmer's disease, isn't it?'

Unsporting of him, he knew, but he couldn't resist saying it.

'Looks that way,' Cruikshank responded. 'Graylaw'd had a

field-day on the literature. And I had to go up there and put down that wretched poodle. I know it wasn't officially diagnosed, but whatever Proctor has, it stuck out a mile that he'd got it too. It would have been madness to leave him at large any longer. Anyway, I'm sending the body to Exleigh for a PM.'

'Oh, hell,' Tim said. 'Did you see Ivy working at the Proctors'?'

'I saw her. I wouldn't say working. She and the unfortunate Proctor girl – Ellen – were huddled in the kitchen drinking tea, and I couldn't say which of them looked the more depressed. I did take the opportunity of asking her whether she'd ever taken the dachshund to work with her, and she swore she hadn't.'

'It's mind-boggling,' said Tim. 'I'm certain Ivy wouldn't lie about that, yet we can presumably take it as read that Fritz has Primmer's too.'

'Well, I should think so, wouldn't you?' Cruikshank dismissed the implied query with contempt.

'Then could that mean that she's a carrier? Or incubating it? Wouldn't a daily help working in a house, touching food and cleaning and possibly using lavatories, be moderately likely to pass it on?'

'Or could it be the other way round? Could Proctor and the poodle have given it one to the other and also to Ivy, who in her turn passed it on to Fritz? If she were in the early stages she might well be quite unaware of it, while it galloped in the dog. Or,' Cruikshank gnawed at his wispy moustache, 'could the lot of them have caught it from another unknown source?'

'Unlikely,' was Tim's opinion, 'in view of what Philip Anstruther told me last night.'

'I think I'll have a word with Peters,' Cruikshank said abruptly. 'Ask him if he can throw any light on all this.'

Which showed Tim how extremely worried he must be, for the Crook and Andrew Peters, the vet in neighbouring Bagthorpe, were incompatible, to put it mildly.

Peters was just about to go out, and in a hurry, as he made abundantly clear when he picked up his receiver.

'No, I haven't heard of any other such cases, but I've had several of your patients here today. That's why I'm running late. Scared to darken your doors, they said.'

'Is that so?' Cruikshank's already reddish face grew redder. 'Well, if that's how they feel, you're welcome to them!'

'Oh, I don't want them, I assure you. As soon as whatever your problem is has been settled you can have the lot of them back. I'm overworked as it is. This isn't a refugee camp!'

'You heard all that, I take it?' said Cruikshank, replacing his own receiver with a good deal more force than necessary. 'Filthy fellow!'

Tim nodded. 'I should think they could have heard it halfway down the road. Still, what can one expect from a pig but a grunt?' Any doubts he might have had as to the wisdom of that remark were dissipated by the look it earned him from his superior.

'There's someone at the door,' he said a moment later. 'Must be an emergency.'

It was Ivy Miller, and inevitably she was weeping.

'I saw both your cars outside. I had to speak to you.'

'Come in.' To Tim's amazement Cruikshank went over to a cupboard from whose depths he brought forth two bottles and a glass. 'A brandy and soda may help. I take it the news is bad?'

She gulped and nodded.

'I rang up about Fritz at dinner time when my hubby was home. It was that horrible thing they're all talking about, I suppose. Primmer's, they called it.'

The long and short of it was that she had had to agree to have him put down.

'He had all sorts of tubes stuck in him they said, so he wouldn't notice the difference when . . .' Another gulp.

'I know,' said Cruikshank with uncharacteristic gentleness. 'Go on, drink that. They were right, you know. It was much the kindest thing to do. He wouldn't have known anything about it, I promise you.'

'Poor old Ivy,' said Tim, quite forgetting to call her Mrs Miller. Believe me, we do know how you feel.'

'Ta,' she said. 'And for the brandy. But the thing I really came to tell you was that, though I wasn't lying when I said I'd never taken Fritz to work, them two dogs did meet. In the park. And they had a fight. Quite a bad one.'

'What?'

'Yes. I was walking Fritz there one afternoon. We met Humphrey out on his own, and he knew me, you see. And he went for Fritz. Always very jealous and aggressive he was.'

'And you didn't mention it to the Proctors at the time?'

'No, I didn't, because I knew it meant that someone, maybe me, maybe one of the family, must have left the garden gate open, and if Mr Proctor had found out about it he would have been that angry. So I just picked Fritz up – he was bleeding, mind you – and walked Humphrey back to the house and made him go in. There wasn't much wrong with him.'

'How long ago was this, then?'

'I can't remember exactly. Ten months to a year maybe.'

'But you didn't say anything about it this morning?' Tim probed gently. 'Or did you tell Mrs Proctor after Mr Cruikshank had left?'

'No. I didn't know what to do, see.' She looked at Cruikshank. 'It wasn't that I didn't understand what you was getting at when you asked me if I'd ever taken him up there, but it's all been so confusing and upsetting and I couldn't bear for that poor girl to think that Fritz and I were the cause of her hubby's illness.' So she had seen the possible connection. 'And losing the dog too. So I thought it was best to come to you. You'd know what to do.'

More moved by this touching confession than either would have cared to admit, the two men looked at each other.

'Well, I don't know, Ivy.' As the one who knew her better Tim felt it was up to him to do the talking. 'But after what you've just told us, my guess is that it was the other way round and Fritz caught it from Humphrey.' Of Walter Proctor he made no mention. Any comments on his condition could come only from Graylaw. One thing he did ask, though.

'Assuming, as I think we have to do, that Mr Proctor caught this disease from Humphrey, is there any way you can account for it? You see it appears that, in this climate, at any rate, it can only be passed on through fairly intimate contact with a victim. Yet Mr Proctor doesn't sound the type of person to make a great deal of fuss of a pet.' Not like you, he refrained from saying.

'No, he didn't and that's the truth. He liked Humphrey all right, more than that poor cat he had put down, but Humphrey did have a habit of spraying all over the place, indoors, I mean, when the mood took him. To show who was boss was what I always thought. He didn't do it in front of Mr Proctor, though.'

Sensible Humphrey, thought Tim.

'So who used to mop it up when this happened?'

'Oh, Mrs Proctor or me. She was always a bit particular about wearing rubber gloves, though. Still, I suppose Mr Proctor could have touched something without realizing.'

'Uh-huh,'commented Tim. 'Touching wouldn't be enough, though. He'd have had to drink from a contaminated glass or something like that.'

'Yes?' said Ivy. 'Well, he might have done at that. Quite fond of his glass is Mr Proctor.' Taking a sip from her own, she blurted out, 'I think I've got it too, you know. That's to say I think Dr Graylaw does.' Her tear-filled eyes looked pleadingly up at Tim as if for reassurance.

'Oh? Has he said so?'

She shook her head.

'Not in so many words he hasn't, but he's making a lot more of my stiff leg than he did before all this happened. Humphrey limped, you see, and so does Mr Proctor. And he says that Mrs Proctor and I must go to Bristol to be tested. And my Ned too. He isn't at all pleased about that, I can tell you, though he does say he'll drive us there.'

'Oh dear.' Realizing that his assistant was at a loss how to reply, Cruikshank tried to come to the rescue. 'Poor Mrs Miller. Troubles never come singly, do they? But I'm sure you've no need to worry. It's only common sense for the three of you to be tested in the circumstances and a limp doesn't have to mean anything, particularly in this changeable weather.' He drew a deep breath. 'And if by some remote chance any of you should prove positive, you'd be all right, you know. As I've discovered only too recently, there's no problem about treating Primmer's disease in the early stages. Now cheer up, drink up and have the other half.'

Tim could hardly believe his ears.

'Go on, Ivy,' he urged. 'Mr Cruikshank's right. It's what you need just now. And then I'll drive you home.'

For one horribly embarrassing moment he thought she was going to kiss him.

16

Although all Tim's instincts had been preparing him for Ivy's miserable news, its actual confirmation had really shaken him. Cruikshank was shaken too, but much luckier in that he was unaware of Tim's guilty secret.

After he had dropped her, at least temporarily tranquillized, in Jubilee Crescent he forced himself out to endure three routine calls, one to a private house, two to farms, then worked doggedly through the queue of evening surgery patients, fewer than he would normally have expected, which in itself was all too significant.

At the end it was Cruikshank, looking definitely the worse for wear, who said, 'Hadn't you better be getting off home now, before some fresh disaster strikes?'

'I shall in a minute,' Tim agreed. 'I've just the odd thing to sort out first.'

By this time Angela was back at her mopping up.

'I must say one does see Marjorie's point about "contaminated premises",' she said, wrinkling her nose in distaste at a fairly extensive, yellowish puddle on the linoleum.

'You know quite well that's not what she was getting at,' he answered irritably. 'That'll only have been Mr Hunter's old Airedale. Look, Angela, I've a nasty feeling that this whole business is getting out of control. I daren't waste any more time. I've got to do something about the Binding cat tonight.'

'Oh yeah? How?'

'It's half past six. I'm going to ring Mrs Binding now and ask if she can bring him along straight away. After all, it's only just round the corner. I think I've worked out a fairly convincing line of sales talk, but I do need you to help keep her away from me while I'm taking the sample. Can you stay?'

'I reckon so. Life's pretty quiet just now with Bruce away.'

'Then what I'd like you to do is produce one of those leaflets over there for her to see – the ones about insurance – and discuss the pros and cons. We can think of some while she's on the way here.'

'Assuming she agrees to come.'

'Well, obviously. And put most of them somewhere out of sight. If she sees how many there are, she'll just decide to take one home to read and come in with the cat. When she arrives – assuming she does, as you say – I shall be moderately brusque and authoritative and whip him into the Crook's room. You can't hear so many noises off from there.'

'But can you hold him down without any help?'

'I'll have to. Shove his head under my arm, I suppose. And it's going to mean shaving him too. I'll have to take quite a lot of blood.'

'But won't she spot that?'

'She may well, but there's no avoiding it. I'll just have to be darned careful. Now you're moderately well acquainted with her and she always seems to like you, so if the insurance discussion runs out of steam you'll have to dredge up some kind of girlish chit-chat.'

'Girlish? With Mrs B.?'

'Oh, don't be so difficult! Frumpy old middle-aged woman chat, if you prefer it. But just take darned good care she doesn't suspect you of being up to anything. If things go wrong, I'm the one who's responsible. Don't compromise yourself. And don't be snide either!' he ended as she responded by whistling the melody of *My Hero* from *The Chocolate Soldier.* Angela was a staunch supporter of the Somerstrand Operatic Society.

George Binding, audibly eating, answered the telephone and, sounding surprised, went off to fetch his wife.

'Hello!' She too sounded startled. 'Mr Proud?'

'Yes, hello. I hope this isn't a bad time for me to be ringing you, but surgery's finished fairly early this evening and it seemed a good opportunity to check up on one or two of my recent patients. How's Orestes? Is his ear healing up nicely?'

'Oh.' She took a moment or two to think about it. 'Yes, I suppose so, though actually it does still seem to be rather sore and inflamed, probably because he will keep on scratching it. There's really no way of stopping him.'

'M'm. I expect you're right, but would you care to bring him along now for me to have a quick look? Just to make sure. And I can probably give him something to ease the itching. No extra charge for the visit, of course; you've already paid.'

'Oh!' she repeated, more taken aback than ever. 'That's very kind of you. I can certainly do that. In about ten minutes?'

'Right,' said Tim. 'Fine.' He turned to Angela. 'His ear's sore. That's one bit of luck. Ten minutes, she said.'

The luck held, though to what extent Angela was uncertain when she opened the outside door to find herself confronted by George, alone save for the occupant of the cat-carrier he was holding.

'My wife got held up,' he explained. 'Unexpected telephone call from her sister. They'll probably still be talking when I get back. You know how it is.'

Handing the carrier to an immensely relieved Tim, who came out to meet him, he flopped onto one of the waiting-room benches and made no attempt to follow him any further.

As he waited, George seemed restless and ill at ease.

'There's a strange sort of atmosphere in the town at the moment,' he said at length to Angela, who had seen no reason to pursue the farce of the pet-insurance leaflets and was now fiddling with her files. 'You'll know what it's all about, of course.'

'Oh, that! Yes, I really think everyone's gone crazy.' She

dimpled encouragingly at him. 'It's amazing how het up people get if they imagine there's some kind of nasty illness going around. Out of all proportion to the facts. How did you come to hear about it, Mr Binding?'

'At the golf-club this evening. And when my wife was having her hair done this afternoon nobody at the place could talk about anything else, she said.'

'Honestly!' Angela laughed. 'It makes one think of that whispering game children play at parties. Remember?'

George did.

'So, seriously, you don't think there's any reason for us to worry?'

'I can't see why. All I know is what I've heard from the vets here, but whatever it is does seem to involve only two households. Of course it was very unfortunate that Mrs Henshaw had to listen in on a private conversation and make a meal of it. She's been dismissed for scaremongering, did you know? I'm doing the cleaning until they find someone else.'

'Ah,' he said gloomily.

'Anyway, why don't you ask Mr Proud about it? He knows far more than I do. He shouldn't be a minute now.'

In fact it was another three before Tim emerged, looking happier.

'Here he is again, Mr Binding. All yours. The abscess is fine. The ear is slightly inflamed but, as your wife said, that's probably due to the scratching. If you put a little of this antiseptic powder on it at intervals that should help, and I've cut his claws as well. Perhaps not to be recommended in normal circumstances, but we do want to minimize any scratching.'

George took the carrier.

'Thank you very much. My wife will be grateful too. Just one thing, though. Could I . . ?'

'Speak to me in private? Yes, of course. Come in here for a moment.' He led the way back into the recently vacated consulting-room.

'I don't want you to take this amiss.' The older man was painfully embarrassed. 'I was just wondering – well, there wasn't anything else behind your ringing my wife, was there? Apart from the reason you gave?'

That was a nasty and quite unexpected shock.

'No, of course not.' Tim smiled, hoping that the sudden hammering of his heart wasn't actually audible. 'What other reason could there be?' Certainly not a secret passion for Priscilla, he thought wildly, and suppressed a hysterical laugh.

'I don't know. Something to do with those rumours that are going round, I suppose. Orestes. Did you think he might somehow have contracted this disease, plague or whatever?'

'But why ever should he?'

Might he be forgiven, Tim prayed.

'Well, sore ears are apparently a symptom, so they say.'

'Yes, but we know quite well how he came by that, not to mention the abscess. In what must have been a first-class catfight.'

'True. Just that it seemed a little unusual for a vet to make the first move, as you did tonight. Very kind, of course.'

'Not at all,' said Tim. 'One does feel concern. I mightn't have got round to it had I been busier, but I do suspect that the rumours are preventing people from coming round here unless they're desperate. All in all, it's a pretty bad scenario.'

'It must be. Well, I really am sorry, Mr Proud. It wasn't your integrity I was doubting, you realize, and I said nothing about this to my wife. No point in worrying her unnecessarily.'

'No, none,' Tim agreed hollowly. 'Absolutely not.'

17

Clare hadn't been very long home from the office when the telephone rang. It was Alison, with whom, due to Rodrigo's illness, she had had no contact for quite some time.

'Clare,' she began without preamble, 'sorry to bother you, but I'm in an awful mess. Rupert's had an accident.'

'What's happened? Where is he?'

'Somewhere outside Perpignan and I can't discover what's happened. Something to do with that damned HGV, I imagine. They rang me up from the hospital where they've got him, and their English was so awful that I couldn't make out anything, and my French is non-existent. You can manage French, can't you?'

'I should think so. Have you the telephone number?'

'No, but I've got the name of the hospital, so I can get it from international enquiries.'

'All right. You do that now, and I'll be straight over.'

'I tried to ring Rupert's boss at his home,' a white-faced Alison told her twenty minutes later, while the children, a boy and girl in their early teens, hovered anxiously behind, 'but he was out, so all I could do was leave a message on his answering-machine. And I've got the number of the hospital.'

'OK.'

Clare wasted no time in initiating the call. It proved a distressingly suspenseful one; the hospital receptionist put her through to someone else and the someone else to a nurse on Rupert's ward, who in her turn had to fetch the ward sister, evidently the only one with the authority to divulge any information.

The accident had had nothing to do with the HGV. Rupert had been sitting at a table outside a café when an elderly motorist had somehow lost control of his car and mounted the pavement. As a result Rupert had a quite badly broken leg and slight concussion, but his condition was in no way life-threatening.

This Clare relayed to Alison before asking how long he was likely to have to stay in the hospital.

'We're to ring again tomorrow. Then they'll be able to tell us more.'

Alison nodded.

'And you don't think they could have been playing it down?'

'I'm sure they weren't. The sister couldn't have sounded more casual. All in a day's work, I should think.'

'Thank God at least for that. Clare, I'm so very grateful to you. Let's all have something to eat now, shall we? The three of us were far too scared to be hungry, and you can't have had time to get your meal. And what about Rodrigo?' she asked a few minutes later as she dished out ham salad. 'I can't think it's good news, not after your long silence.'

'No, I'm afraid not. He died a little while ago.'

'Then what was it?' Alison's expression conveyed enough sympathy to make further words unnecessary.

'Some weird parasitic thing he must somehow have picked up in Spain.' Clare had long since decided not to burden her with worries about the possible spread of infection, nor the fact that on advice given at the veterinary hospital she had gone for a blood test and was now awaiting the result. It wasn't as if Rodrigo's unhappy fate could be reason enough for closing the kennels.

'I just wish there were some way of getting to Rupert,' Alison lamented after a while, 'but it's out of the question. That's one of the snags about running a place like this.'

'Well, is it out of the question?' Clare had been thinking about that one. 'If Pam and Jane could keep things going in the daytime throughout the week, I could come in each night to sleep and be here all weekend, which is when most of the changeovers happen, isn't it? I'm not suggesting that you two couldn't cope on your own,' she added hastily to the children, 'but the owners could make out that there should be someone older on the premises.'

'And some of them can be rather tricky to deal with,' Alison supported her. 'And there'd be a certain amount of simple book-keeping to do and the register to keep. Clare, would you really? That would be wonderful. I know my passport's still valid and if he's in plaster and on crutches, as he's bound to be, he really could do with someone to travel home with him.'

'There's one thing that's worrying me; I've only just thought of it,' Clare continued. 'The hospital wanted you to ring in the afternoon and I don't see how I can do that. Things at work have become very difficult recently, and I don't think I dare ask to leave early.'

Especially not after the fuss made by Barnet when she had asked to have time off for the blood test.

'Don't worry about that.' Alison was beginning to look almost cheerful. 'They can do it from Rupert's office, I know. They have to make foreign calls all the time and they'll need to do something about getting the truck back fast because it will be loaded with perishable stuff. What's wrong at work, though? You always seemed so happy there.'

'We've got a foul new manager who apparently wants my job for his girlfriend. And from the way things are going, I've a nasty feeling he's going to get it.'

At that point the doorbell rang.

'It's Mr Foster,' said Alison's Patrick, peering through the window. 'I'll let him in.'

Rupert's employer was a pleasant looking, solid kind of man in his forties, plainly distressed by the message he had found on his answering-machine.

'I've only just got home,' he explained. 'I'm so very sorry, Alison. We'll have to try to find out what's happened.'

'We have,' she told him. 'That's to say my friend, Clare Forrester, has.' She nodded towards Clare. 'She speaks French and she rang the hospital.'

'And?'

'It isn't too bad, relatively. He has a broken leg and concussion, but he's going to be all right. And the truck's all right too; it wasn't involved at all, though I'm afraid you'll have to send someone out to bring it home.'

'That's no great problem. It won't be the first time. What are they doing about Rupert, then? Did they say how long he'd be in hospital?'

'We shan't know till tomorrow afternoon. They asked Clare to ring again then, but her boss won't like her taking the time off for that, so I wondered if that girl of yours would mind doing it? Actually, Clare's offered to sleep here, as well as doing the whole of the weekend stint, so I could go over to fetch him if that seemed a good idea.'

'Sounds the ideal answer. But do you really think you could cope?' he asked Clare.

'Well, I'm an ex-client, you see. My dog – I've just lost him – was a day-boy, so to speak, for over eighteen months, so I'm pretty familiar with the set-up. And of course I'd have Patrick and Anne to supervise me, wouldn't I?'

The children made no objection, in fact they looked quite pleased at the idea.

'The only thing, Alison, is that you would have to get it across to Pam and Jane that they simply must be here in the mornings in time for me to get to work by nine. If I'm late my head will roll.'

'Yes, what is this?' Alison demanded. 'You were saying – well, I thought you were always very happy at that place.'

'Oh, I was till a couple of months ago when the old manager left and this rather frightful new one took over.'

'And he wants your job for his girlfriend? How can he possibly work that? Mr Charters – isn't that his name – would surely never let him.'

'It's not worth worrying about it now.' Embarrassed, Clare gave a little shrug. 'It's just that I'm not allowed to use Catalan any more – she doesn't speak it – and instead of my going to the Barcelona Trades Fair this summer, as I did last, she's going to be there to do the interpreting. And she may come in to do some of my letters in the evenings when I'm on holiday. Various boring things like that.'

'But what's Mr Charters thinking about?'

'I don't know. The line of least resistance, I imagine. He's struck me as being a bit under the weather lately. Anyway, please don't let's waste time talking about all that now. You and Mr Foster have quite enough problems of your own.'

'True.' Foster looked approvingly and with a certain interest at her. 'But you're certainly doing a lot to help solve them. So if you come to the office tomorrow afternoon, Alison, we'll make that call and then try to see about organizing your trip. After which we'll contact you, Miss Forrester. At home,' he added with a smile.

'Fine,' she agreed with an answering one. 'Well, I'll be off now. And thanks for the supper, Alison.'

At least the children weren't going to be difficult, she thought with relief as Patrick escorted her with the utmost courtesy to the door.

18

There were times when George Binding asked himself what on earth Priscilla and he were doing together in a four-foot-six bed. This was one of them.

'What's the matter?' he enquired wearily in the small hours of that particular morning as she turned over for at least the tenth time in as many minutes and a strong, if accidental, kick came his way. 'Something on your mind?'

'Yes. Orestes and that young vet. My every instinct tells me that there's something peculiar going on, something that boy doesn't want us to know. The trouble is, no matter how hard I try, I can't imagine what.'

'M'm. All right then, let's have it.'

Glancing furtively at the morning tea tray on the table beside Priscilla, he abandoned any hope of further sleep.

'Well, I told you how strangely he behaved when I first took Orestes to the surgery after the fight. Practically threw me in via the back door ahead of people who should really have been taken first, then seemed to be using some kind of delaying tactics until he suddenly decided to bundle me out again.'

'M'm.'

'And then doesn't it strike you as rather odd that he should ring up out of the blue and invite me to take him back for a check-up out of surgery hours? And without charging for it, what's more!'

'M'm.' Could a four-foot-six bed in some way be conducive to telepathy, he began to wonder. 'Yes, I do see all that. But on the other hand there's no way that he can know anything about Orestes that we don't. We don't know where he came from, of course, but we've had him for a long time now. And there was nothing particularly unusual about the abscess and the ear. That sort of thing is apt to happen in cat-fights, dammit!'

Dammit, he thought, shocked. What kind of influence was his second wife beginning to exert upon him?

'What I have is a nasty kind of feeling that it has something to do with that dog scare that's going on all over the town. But what, that's the point.'

'But it is only dogs.'

'Uh-huh. But what about that man from up the hill, the one whose poodle had to be put down? They're saying he's got the same thing, you know.'

'Well,' George tried to suppress a renewed twinge of an anxiety which he saw no point in sharing with Priscilla, 'I think there's an awful lot of nonsense being spread about, you know. The whole thing has been blown up out of all proportion. You get that in a little place like this; too many retired people without enough to do.'

'It's not only retired people, I can tell you. It's going on in the shops, at street corners, everywhere. You can sense it. No, I really think I've got to have it out with Mr Proud.'

'Er,' George wriggled and cleared his throat, 'well, my dear, I wasn't going to say anything about it, but I don't think you can. Because I already have.'

'What?' She sat bolt upright. 'You've done what? You never said anything about it!'

'No, because I didn't see any point in worrying you. It was just that like you I did think it all a little strange, so I put it to him as gently as possible and he took it very well. My impression, though he didn't actually say so, was that he's afraid that all this dog fuss is going to do no good to the practice, so he's pulling out all the stops to make sure that no one can point the finger at him about anything else. He seems a decent young fellow, in fact I felt quite sorry for him. I'm sure we needn't worry about Orestes.'

We, thought Priscilla with an unexpected glow. Her husband was definitely improving.

19

As Edward Charlton, Vicar of Somerstrand, strode towards his vestry door that Sunday morning, a stride being just about the most restrained gait he could manage in his present mood, he passed several small clusters of people, some known to him only by sight, chattering like magpies upon the churchyard path. No doubt about what, he thought angrily as he donned his surplice, rounded up his little choir, the bell ceased ringing and about half the gossipers outside came scurrying in for the service.

Charlton was a moderate kind of man in his mid-forties, caring of his flock and unstinting with parish visits and cooperation over local events. The older generation liked him because he indulged them not infrequently with the old traditional eleven o'clock Morning Prayer and had been heard to say that he didn't see why anyone who didn't want to should feel pressurized into shaking hands and exchanging grimaces with total strangers in neighbouring pews, these usually tourists in the summer season. The young liked him too, though even after several months he had yet to be forgiven by certain organizers of the local Cubs and Brownies for having vetoed their All Saints' Day pageant, which was to have been staged in the church hall.

'Well, what else could I do?' he had complained to his wife after attending the dress rehearsal. 'Whatever view you may take of the saints in general, you have to accord them a certain respect, and the whole thing was degenerating into sheer farce.' He snorted. 'Imagine it – Saint Sebastian like a grinning hedgehog and Guy Fawkes bringing up the rear.'

'And he isn't even a saint,' she said seriously.

'Quite.'

This morning he was tight-lipped, white with suppressed rage. His congregation was not to know that his daughter had come home weeping after a school hockey match the previous afternoon claiming that the mothers of several of her classmates were saying that in view of recent events in the town he and his wife ought to set an example to local dog owners by having their collie put down. It had taken the two of them a long time to reassure her and her small brother, and they were still feeling the after-effects. Now somehow, watched anxiously by his wife, he ploughed through the first part of the service with apparent tranquillity.

Then came his sermon.

'My text for today,' he announced, the hint of a tremor in his voice, 'comes from the Book of Job, Chapter thirty-five, verse six: "He multiplieth words without knowledge".'

And the glare with which he raked his hearers left them in no doubt that he meant it personally.

'Seems it's going to be topical,' a woman in front of the Bindings murmured audibly to her companion, while on the other side of the aisle a sharp-faced young man in a dingy brown suit brought surreptitiously from his pocket a small pad and a Biro and looked up with eager concentration.

It was quite some sermon, as well it might be, having taken Charlton half the night to compose.

This last week in Somerstrand, he told them, had seen, to his shock and disbelief, half the town in the throes of what he could only describe as a mindless panic attack, a bout of mass hysteria which could never have occurred had those who started it and others who fuelled it paused to reflect on such facts as they already had before inventing more, used their natural, God-given intelligence instead of spreading wildly sensational rumours, causing added anxiety and distress to those who were already in trouble and stirring it up in others who had not the slightest genuine cause for concern.

At this certain members of his captive audience stirred uneasily.

'The fact, at any rate to my knowledge,' he went on, 'is that two families, and only two in the whole of this community, are suffering the sad consequences of illnesses which may or may not be connected. Much more alarming incidents occur almost everywhere all the time and pass unrecorded, save by the victims, for the simple reason that they have escaped the notice of the eavesdroppers of society, the spiteful, the hysterical, the gossips, or possibly just because something more interesting is going on elsewhere at the time.'

More wriggling, some resentful, Priscilla sensed.

He did not know how many of them had yet heard of the deplorable incident down at the harbour the previous Friday evening, two days ago, when a perfectly blameless young yachtsman staying at nearby Watchet had come ashore with his dog and been set upon, verbally only, he thanked Heaven, by about six passers-by, who were well on the way to developing into a lynch mob before the harbour-master and two other respected members of the community had intervened and managed to restore order. To him, Edward Charlton, the whole incident was reminiscent of the witch-hunts of the Middle Ages.

This said, he was glad to be able to add that there was a happier side to the sorry tale. The poor lady who had been the prime target of so much unkindness had also, she had told him, received sympathy and encouragement from a number of sources, some of them totally unexpected. In this respect the whole wretched affair had surely shown up the difference between the sheep and the goats of the community.

He ended his homily with the optimistic, if not wholly convincing reflection that with the help of grace and considerable, yes, considerable personal effort, the goats of Somerstrand might one day – he was just about to say 'blossom' when he caught a warning glance from his wife and hastily modified it to 'evolve' into sheep. In a manner of speaking, that was.

So saying, 'And now to God the Father . . . ,' he intoned, after which goats and sheep alike rose to join in the singing of 'He Who Would Valiant Be', and any faint and reprehensible sniggers occasioned by the line referring to 'dismal stories' were drowned by the sounds of even the goats letting rip over what they all would have admitted was a rattling good tune.

'Whew!' someone was heard to say as they all emerged into the sunlight. 'Pity old Marge Henshaw's a Methodist.'

'Ah, but she'll be hearing all about it, never fear,' his companion reassured him. 'Plus a bit added on, I'll be bound.'

'So straight to The George and Dragon?' George Binding asked as he prepared to start the car. On Sundays they almost always lunched there. 'Or did you say you had to ring Eileen first?'

'I'm afraid I'll have to. We never did quite settle on the date she was to come, so she'll probably be hanging around waiting for the call. Sorry, dear.'

'Never mind.' Though fond enough of his sister-in-law, George preferred to be fond of her from a distance. Still, he supposed he could put up with her for a week, not that he had much alternative.

'That man in church,' he said eventually after the matter had been finalized to the satisfaction of the two women. 'Did you notice him? The one in the brown suit just in front of us to the left? I think he must have been some kind of journalist. He was scribbling away all through the sermon.'

'No, I can't say I did.' Straightening her hat, she headed for the door and out to the car. 'All I really noticed was how furious the vicar was. He's obviously been having a rough time over all this business, poor man.'

The delay caused by the telephoning resulted in their being rather too late at the pub for comfort, eventually finding themselves at a cramped little corner table with a meal that had spent rather too long on hold. The lounge bar was crammed to capacity and the volume of noise considerable. As he stood waiting, one of a group of several, to give his order to the fortunately unflappable landlord working behind the bar, one nearby conversation, or rather near-monologue, caught his ear.

'It was a great big snake, I'm telling you,' a little fat man was insisting to a visibly sceptical audience. 'Thick as a man's arm and long with it. Slithering along that bit of scrub between the beach and the railway line. You know where I mean, just near Brown's Café. I shouldn't have liked to come face to face with a thing like that, I can tell you.'

'How much did you put in it?' George's neighbour asked the landlord ironically.

'Only the usual,' he was told. 'No, actually,' he frowned as a froth of beer overflowed from the glass he was filling, 'I wouldn't disbelieve it at all, in fact I remember hearing a similar tale a few years back. It probably came off the *Fairlight;* she comes regularly into Watchet from Algeria or somewhere like that with a cargo of esparto grass for the paper mills. A snake could easily get in amongst that and not be noticed, I should think.'

'Nasty.' The man on George's other side shuddered. 'I'd better warn the missus not to walk the dog down there.'

'Well, 'twon't survive the winter, that's for sure,' someone else remarked. ''Twould never stand up to the climate.'

That subject exhausted and several more customers attended to, while George noticed that across the room Priscilla had finally succeeded in taking possession of the corner table, he learned that the man in the brown suit had been in earlier, eating cold pork pie, drinking beer, of which he had actually stood a round, and asking a whole lot of questions about the events of the past week. They all agreed that, even though he hadn't said so, he had to have been a reporter of some kind.

'Local, do you think?' George queried.

'Couldn't have been,' someone replied. 'We were at church – he was too, you know – and my wife heard him asking the way to Cheddar Close. No local would have needed to do that.'

'Cheddar Close, did you say?' A youngish man just moving off turned sharply, almost spilling his beer.

'That's right. Mean something to you?'

'I'm afraid it could do. It's worth following up, anyway.' His expression was grim, and he ignored the questioner's tacit appeal to say more.

'Now who was that?' George demanded. 'I'm sure I've seen him around.'

'Him? That's Mike Carpenter. Teaches up at the Comp.'

'I don't like it.' Opening a door behind him for the umpteenth time, the landlord yelled, 'Two beef and Yorkshire, Mary. No, not one little bit. Wild stories about infectious diseases are the last thing we want in a seaside resort like this. It could ruin trade for the whole of the rest of the summer. No, the local boys would have more sense than to write up a story like this, even for the sake of a scoop.'

'Yet this chap must have had some kind of advance inside information,' George persisted, thankful that food did really seem at last to be in the offing. 'Why else would he have gone to the church with his notebook and so forth? He was expecting the vicar to say something, no doubt about that. I was watching him.'

'Ah, but only the vicar himself could have known what the sermon was going to be about,' someone objected.

'Only the vicar would have known precisely.' Wiping his brow, the landlord took a deep swallow from the glass beside him. 'But there's plenty of folks round here with a pretty good idea of the sort of thing he'd be likely to do in a situation like this. When he's really rattled he doesn't mince his words. He speaks his mind.'

'Even to the town's disadvantage,' someone else said glumly.

'But surely it wasn't to the disadvantage of the tourist industry,' George said, 'in that he rather scotched the whole story? Or at least,' he reflected again, 'no harm would have been done if there hadn't been some newshound in the congregation all set to make what he could of it. So as it was, I suppose,' he conceded, 'in all innocence the vicar handed it to him on a plate.'

20

Within forty-eight hours of hearing the news about Rupert, Alison had taken off for France and Clare found herself in charge of the kennels.

'I hope I'm doing all right,' she confided to Paul over Alison's telephone, 'but what with one thing and another it feels a bit like walking a tightrope.'

The children were friendly, obviously appreciating that she consulted them rather than attempting to exert the slightest authority, and Pam was perfectly cooperative. Jane she knew disliked her, admittedly with some cause, and would arrive for work each morning at the last possible moment.

'Is she still going strong with Harold?' she enquired of Pam.

'Oh yes, thick as thieves, but he's away on some job at the moment.'

So the brinkmanship in the mornings had to be sheer badness. Just as long as she didn't decide to go sick, Clare thought nervously. That really would put the cat among the pigeons.

There was one woman, a day-dog owner, who was definitely a nuisance. Clare had met her several times in the past when delivering or collecting Rodrigo, and had realized that she was something of a 'buttonholer', to use one of her own expressions. Probably the woman was lonely, which was sad, but there was an intensity about her, a speculative air that grated on Clare's nerves. 'She makes me feel like an insect under a microscope,' she had once said laughingly to Alison.

Now she found herself to a certain extent at her mercy, no longer in a position to slip away with a vague smile.

'So you've taken over, have you?' Miss Tennant commented with her disconcerting stare. 'What a responsibility! I think you're very brave. Don't you?' It didn't sound exactly like a compliment.

'Oh, it won't be for long,' Clare responded brightly. 'I've got the girls behind me and I really couldn't have let Alison down. After all, I'd been coming here for quite a time and I suppose one could say that I know the ropes.'

'Yes, I was wondering about that. I haven't seen you recently. Has something happened to your little dog?'

The question Clare most dreaded against the present background. If a smuggled Spanish pup had posed a threat to the kennels, Rodrigo's story could well provide a worse one.

'Yes, I lost him a little while back. It was very sad.'

'Oh, I'm sorry.' The woman's air of curiosity increased. 'But he was quite young, wasn't he? Whatever happened?'

'Something intestinal. The vet did explain at the time, but it was rather technical for me. I just try not to think about it.'

This at least did have the desired effect, at any rate for the present, and Clare was free at last to drive to the office as fast as she dared. Had she not been lucky over traffic-lights nothing could have saved her from playing into Barnet's hands by being late.

There the cold war, as she thought of it, and not always so cold at that, seemed to be intensifying, probably because Charters was away ill, which left Barnet with greater responsibility and more opportunities for making himself unpleasant.

On Clare's fourth morning as Alison's stand-in Pam rang her up at about coffee break time to tell her that one of the boarding dogs had developed what sounded ominously like kennel-cough. She had already moved him into an isolation area, but what next?

'Just ring the vet, I should think,' Clare advised. 'You're

entitled to do that. And meanwhile look in the records to see if he's been vaccinated against it. Because I don't think that's one Alison insists on.'

'And what was that?' asked Barnet, coming into her room just as she was ringing off. 'Nothing to do with that missing consignment, I take it?'

'No.' She had no alternative but to explain, causing him to frown and look pointedly at his watch.

'I see. By the way, all this drove it from my mind, but I just dropped in to mention that there was a phone call for you earlier on from the Springfield Hospital.'

'Oh.' Clare's heart seemed to miss a beat. 'But you didn't put it through to me. Was there any message?'

'Not really. I did explain that you were busy just then, and whoever it was – Dr Someone-or-other – you'll know the name presumably – asked if you could go along to see him around six this evening. He said he wouldn't be available till then, so there's no point in trying to ring him back. It will be in connection with that blood test you had, I imagine.'

'So should I,' she said, 'which is why it would have been preferable not to have to wait until six o'clock to hear.'

Predictably this drew not the slightest reaction from her tormentor.

At lunchtime she telephoned Pam, who reported that the vet's verdict had been that the dog did indeed have a mild attack of kennel-cough in spite of having been vaccinated, but that in view of the layout of the establishment and her own quick action it was unlikely to develop into a serious outbreak. And yes, she would stay on until Clare returned from the hospital.

'Try not to worry, Clare,' said Anna a little later, having overheard the exchange with Barnet through Clare's open door. 'I know you told me they weren't going to contact you unless the result was positive, but it could well be something else which that sadistic so-and-so decided to suppress.'

'M'm.'

'Well, you've never had any symptoms, have you?'

'Probably not. Apart from a wild, furious, passionate desire to do something quite awful to Barnet.'

It would take her the best part of an hour to get to the hospital on the far side of the town and at four o'clock she put on her jacket and walked out without a word to him.

'If he asks where I am,' she told Sybil as she passed her desk, 'just tell him that if he'd had the common decency to put a certain telephone call through to me this morning, I shouldn't have to be leaving now.'

'Wow!' Sybil raised her brows and blinked theatrically. 'Like that, is it? Well, the best of luck anyway!'

The Springfield Hospital for Infectious Diseases was quiet when Clare arrived, reminding her that it was not the kind of institution one would expect to find teeming with visitors at six o'clock in the evening. A slightly surprised nurse ushered her into the sanctum of Dr Smethers, a tall, thin, youngish man whom they found riffling through a pile of loose papers in anxious search of something, to judge from the dishevelled appearance of his hair.

'Oh hello there, Miss Forrester.' As he bundled the papers into a drawer and rose to pull out a chair for her before sitting down again himself, he gave the impression of mild surprise. 'Good of you to come all this way when you could have telephoned.'

'Could I? But didn't you say I was to come?'

'Well, I didn't put it quite so strongly as that, but I must admit it's helpful to be able to talk to you face to face. By the way, it was good about your test, wasn't it?'

'What? You mean it was all right?' She could hardly believe her ears.

'Yes, of course. Didn't the man at your office tell you? I certainly asked him to.'

'No, he did not.' Her hands tightened on the bag she held on her lap. 'Oh, that's really too bad of him!'

Smethers stared and shook his head as if in disbelief.

'That's quite extraordinary! Incredibly thoughtless. You

must have had a horrible day, thinking the worst.'

'I did rather, but never mind; it's all over now.'

'It is as far as you're concerned. Which brings me to why I wanted to talk to you. It's wildly unlikely, I know, but I suppose you've never come across a chap called Bert Rollins? From Gateshead. Fellow of about thirty, a factory foreman, apparently.'

That was Clare's second nasty shock of the day. Truthful by nature, the last thing she could afford to do was tell him the whole truth. To give herself time to think she put on a brief show of searching her memory.

'Yes, I think I know who you must mean. I couldn't get it for a moment. I've never actually met him, but Mrs Edenfield has mentioned him.' She paused. 'You wouldn't be going to tell me that he has Primmer's disease?'

He nodded.

'He has, I'm afraid. But what makes you say that?'

'Well, my dog bit him, you see, so I'm told,' she confessed nervously. 'Before he became obviously ill he used to go on working days to Mrs Edenfield's kennels, as you know, and apparently this Mr Rollins went there to see one of the kennel maids about some private matter or other. I don't know the exact details, but he ran into Mrs Edenfield, who had Rodrigo with her at the time, and she and Mr Rollins had a fairly heated argument that ended with him shaking her arm and shouting at her. So Rodrigo tried to protect her. Still, that's awful,' she went on into the non-committal silence with which Smethers received this. 'But he often bit me too, particularly towards the end when he was feeling utterly wretched.'

'Probably only superficially. The bite Rollins got must have been pretty deep.' He picked up a pencil and began to chew it thoughtfully. 'Even so, you were lucky. He did tell me he'd been bitten by a dog, but for some reason he was determined not to say whose or where. So you can thank your lucky stars that he's unlikely to be taking any legal action.'

'No, I don't think he'll be doing that,' she returned a little sharply. 'Will he recover, though, do you think?'

'With luck he should do. He was fortunate enough in that

he had a doctor who didn't take long to realize that he was a case for us. But it certainly won't increase his life expectancy.'

Putting down the pencil, he leant back, eyes narrowed.

'Forgive me, but you wouldn't be hiding something, would you?'

'Of course not. Why do you ask?'

'I don't know; just a feeling. You have an expressive face, and Rollins was definitely cagey about something. I just wondered if you knew what.'

'Well, maybe I do.' Clare's expressive face was now the picture of guilt. 'But I do promise you that it's totally irrelevant to his illness.'

'Can you be sure of that, though?'

'Quite sure. Absolutely certain, in fact.'

'Then I suppose it's no good pressing you further.' Now he was definitely annoyed. 'But there's still the matter of the staff at that kennels. Are any of them at risk, would you say? Because if so, after what you've just told me they'd better come along here pretty damn quick and be tested.'

'I doubt if anyone's at risk,' she told him. 'They didn't have to feed or exercise him, and I'm sure I'd have heard about it if he'd bitten anyone. Still, of course I'll warn them. Actually,' at this point she had decided that a certain candour was the best policy, 'I shall be seeing them tonight. Mrs Edenfield had to go to France for a few days and I'm standing in for her. Helping to, that is.'

This time Smethers literally gaped.

'Full of surprises, aren't you, Miss Forrester?' he said at length. 'Well, I suppose that's just one more reason to be glad your test was negative.'

21

Simon Webster, headmaster of Somerstrand Comprehensive, must have been one of the last inhabitants to hear of the panic currently pervading the town. It was from Mike Carpenter, teacher of English language and literature, that he learnt of it when on the Tuesday following the vicar's outspokenness in church Mike almost burst into his study brandishing a tabloid newspaper which he placed unceremoniously in Simon's desk.

'Mind if I talk to you for a moment?'

'Carry on.'

For some reason, Simon noticed, Mike was also clutching a mottled red exercise book of the kind reserved for the older pupils' English essays.

'You won't have seen this, I take it?'

Mike pointed an accusing finger at a long article on the right-hand side of the tabloid's front page.

Simon looked and shook his head.

'Not my kind of reading. What is it then?' There was a pause while he picked it up and found out. 'Good God! Did you know anything about this? Before this morning, I mean?'

'Well, I'd heard that a handful of local people had worked themselves up into a lather over some weirdo disease from abroad, probably introduced by a dog, but nothing about fights in supermarkets and near lynchings on the quay and fire and brimstone from the pulpit.'

'Um,' said Simon. 'I don't think I like this at all. The kids will have heard about it, I take it?'

'And how! Sole topic of conversation all over the school,

I'm told. We almost had a riot among the third after assembly – non pet owners versus potential plague-spreaders. Seems a lot of the parents read this rag over their cornflakes.'

'But how do you think the paper got onto it, and so quickly? Did some renegade from *The Somerstrand Gazette* sneak it up to London?'

'No, that's the point I'm coming to. My guess is that we'll find the source of the story a whole lot closer to home. Take a look at this.' He opened the exercise book at an essay headed 'Communication in the Community.' 'Now compare some of the phraseology in this with one or two expressions in the paper. I think you'll see what I mean. Look there.' He placed a finger on the newsprint. 'Second paragraph: "Suggestible victims of their own neuroses." That's part of our roving reporter's paraphrase of the vicar's sermon.'

Simon peered.

'Yes, I've got it.'

'And now here, in Frank Parsons's essay, we have "suggestible victims of advertising propaganda".'

'M'm.'

'And there's more. Look at paragraph four. "In present-day society health hazards have become the subject of almost universal concern."'

'Yes.'

'And bloody little Parsons has written, "The almost universal concern engendered by selective emphasis on health hazards . . ."'

'Um. How long ago did Parsons write this?'

Mike flicked over a page.

'It's dated May twenty-fourth – well before all this blew up. And he's aiming to become a journalist, by the way.'

'But he obviously didn't write it all himself. For one thing he wouldn't have had time. He'd have needed to get it into the post by Saturday afternoon, well before the sermon. Plus there's no mention here of his name.'

'True, but I'm pretty sure what happened. I was in The George and Dragon having a drink at lunchtime on Sunday and several blokes at the bar were talking about some newspaper reporter – that's what they all agreed he must have been – who was seen in church taking notes on the sermon, and went on there to ask a whole lot of questions. Unfortunately he'd left before I'd arrived, but – the most interesting thing of all – he evidently asked someone how to get to Cheddar Close which, should you not remember, is where Frank Parsons lives. Which has to mean that he contacted the paper to put them on to what might well have been a scoop, and they sent their man down pronto. Makes sense, wouldn't you say?'

'I suppose it does.' Simon rose and strolled to the window to glance down at the playground from which the noise now arising was even more raucous than usual. 'But what can we do about it, Mike? It wasn't a nice thing to do, particularly in a town like this, but he hasn't committed a crime or even broken any school rules. And the cat, if there really is one, is well and truly out of the bag.'

'Oh, I know.' Mike was so plainly disgruntled that Simon suddenly remembered that his brother-in-law was one of Somerstrand's army of guest-house keepers. 'And this roving reporter character has been extremely careful not to mention any names. I imagine Parsons must also have gone to church, not realizing that the reporter was there, then gone home to write his own version of the article and the newshound lifted the parts of it that suited him. Probably to save time, because he can't have had much.'

'Sounds like it,' Simon agreed. 'So all I can do, I suppose, is have him up and give him a thorough lecture on the evils of ambition when combined with total selfishness. He won't try to deny anything, I imagine?'

'Not a chance!' Mike snorted. 'He'll be far too cock-a-hoop over his little success. Until the backlash hits him, of course. It's strange that he didn't think of that, I must say. Oh blimey,' he too had wandered over to the window, 'do you see what I see?'

'What?'

'Policeman. Our local sarge in full regalia. And heading in this direction.'

As Sergeant Pearson plodded his ponderous way across the

concrete surrounding the school, the milling children, startled and staring, fell back to allow him passage.

'Oh Lord,' Simon groaned. 'Not more shoplifting. I really can't take it.'

'Or vandalism,' Mike added. 'We've had quite enough of that too.'

There he was nearer the mark.

'Ah, good morning,' the sergeant greeted them as the school secretary ushered him into the study. 'Mind if I trouble you for a moment?'

'Not at all, Sergeant.' Simon smiled bravely. 'Sit down, won't you?'

'Well, I'll be off.' Ignoring his superior's semi-appealing glance, Mike headed for the door. 'I've a class in a moment, and you know what IVa's like.'

'All right, Mike.' Simon looked at his watch. 'It's eleven-fifteen now. Could you find Frank Parsons and tell him to come and see me at noon? And leave the – er – papers here.'

'Will do.'

A bright smile and Mike had departed.

This exchange had allowed the sergeant time to take stock of his surroundings.

'Ah,' he said heavily, pointing to the newspaper on the desk. 'So you've seen that then, have you, sir?'

Simon nodded. 'Which means that you have. Would that be what you've come about?'

'Well, only possibly, sir, and very indirectly at that. No, I was just wondering whether you could throw any light on a lad at this school. Sam Cridland.'

'What kind of light?'

'Well, do you think he's the type to go smashing a neighbour's greenhouse?'

'I wouldn't put it past him. He's a pretty rough character. Strictly off the record, of course. Do you think he has, then?'

'It looks very much like it. The greenhouse belongs to the lady mentioned in that paper, the one whose dog seems to have this disease they're all on about. A few nights ago someone climbed into her back garden and threw stones. The Cridland lad lives nearby, and another neighbour, a Mrs Sarah Morrison, and her husband say they saw him and three others running out of the lane behind the garden at approximately the time of the incident. She said they seemed – well – exhilarated, and jeered at the two of them.'

'That sounds like Sam Cridland all right, but you haven't enough proof, have you? Not if they weren't actually seen to do it?'

'No, that's why we haven't taken any action sooner. But I was wondering if you could give him a warning, like. Tell him off about the rudeness to the Morrisons and say this whole business will have done him no good at all if he gets himself into any trouble that can be proved.'

'All right, I suppose I can do that. He probably saw you coming, so I'll let him sweat a bit before I send for him. Did this Mrs Morrison recognize any of the others?'

'No. One had red hair and freckles, she said.'

'Yes, that would be Peter Simms, one of his cronies. I'll send for him too. Any hope of scaring them by saying you may have found traces in the garden?'

'I doubt it.' The sergeant shook his head. 'They'd probably remember that there was quite a lot of rain that night. Still, it's worth a try.'

With which he took his leave, to walk slowly and obviously back through the now deserted playground.

Simon had just time to gulp down the coffee hastily deposited on his desk by the secretary before Frank Parsons put in his appearance. A fresh-faced lad of seventeen, with a shock of wavy fair hair, he seemed totally unaware of any impending trouble, so confident, in fact, that it gradually dawned on Simon that he was expecting to be congratulated on his recent dalliance with the press.

As Simon had intended, he immediately noticed the newspaper.

'You've seen it then, sir?'

'That's why I sent for you.'

Sheer curiosity prompted him to assume a less intimidating manner than he had originally intended.

'But who told you I had a hand in it? It's the reporter who's taken all the credit.'

Considerable disappointment there.

'You told me so yourself,' Simon answered drily.

'Oh?'

At the older man's tone the exuberance faded a little.

'Yes. Mr Carpenter showed me one of your essays – here, you might as well have it back now. Take a look at the one on "Communication in the Community" and compare some of the expressions with certain ones in the article. Too close for coincidence, wouldn't you say? Frankly I consider the style far too high-flown for a paper of this kind, but presumably our roving reporter didn't have time to water it down. You did contact his paper didn't you, and manage to get him sent along here?'

'That's right, sir. What you're saying is that I shouldn't have?'

'What I'm saying is that I'm pretty sure you're going to regret it. I take it the whole school knows about your part in it?'

Parsons reddened.

'Well, probably, sir,' he admitted, looking down at his feet.

'Now tell me,' Simon went on with what he hoped was an effective blend of disapproval and confidentiality, 'how did you come to hear about all this? It was complete news to me.'

Not quite the best way of putting it, he realized too late, but Parsons seemed not to notice.

'Well, the whole town's buzzing with the story. My mother told me about it first, and she kept updating it. She goes shopping and to coffee mornings and so on. You know the kind of thing.'

'And does she think it was a good idea for you to do this?'

The boy gave a faint shrug.

'I don't really know. I suppose she tells my father and me things without taking much notice of our reactions. He tends to switch off and let it go over his head.'

That fitted in pretty well with Simon's recollection of ebullient, swift-speaking Mrs Parsons.

'But how did you find out about the man, whoever he is, who contracted the disease?'

'I didn't. The reporter did that. He rang up on Sunday night and said he'd spoken to various people and they all seemed glad enough to talk.'

That Simon could well believe.

'But they wouldn't have been anyone involved in the tourist industry, one would think.'

Amazingly that was an aspect of the whole affair that seemed to have escaped young Parsons. He hedged.

'I don't really know. He said he couldn't try the doctor, but he did have a go at the vets and they were both pretty rude and unhelpful. So was the husband of the woman whose dog started it all. He was quite threatening, he said. He even thought he might be going to attack him.'

'Well, can you really blame him? Don't you think you've been a bit insensitive, trying to make capital out of other people's suffering, just for the sake of a good story?'

'I suppose I didn't think of it that way.' By now Parsons was scarlet. 'I do want to be a journalist, you know, and it seemed like an opening.'

'Yes, I see that.' Simon relented slightly. 'This won't have got you anywhere, though. By the time you're ready to start work your roving reporter will have roved somewhere else and the editor of the paper won't even have heard of you. Besides, surely you want to go in for something a bit better than this sort of rag?'

Parsons supposed he did.

'Oh well,' Simon ended dismissively, 'you acted on impulse, I suppose, and what's done is done. All I can say to you is keep up with your writing on a more elevated level if you can and if you're hoping for a holiday job this summer, I'd advise you not to try any of the hotels!'

22

'George!' Priscilla's urgent call carried clarion-like from the kitchen to the other side of the house where her husband was standing in gloomy contemplation of the rain-soaked garden. Were they never to have any summer this year? He turned away from the window.

'What is it, dear?'

'Orestes. Just come and look.'

A saturated Orestes was standing resignedly on the kitchen table where Priscilla had placed him to be dried – a practice to which George could never become reconciled. Leaning over him, she had flung down the towel she had been using and was peering closely at one ginger and white striped back leg.

'Just look!' she repeated, her voice rising in outrage. 'I was right. That Proud boy has been up to something.'

George obeyed.

'What do you mean? Oh yes, I see. Well, I don't see why you should say that. He probably did it jumping over a fence or something.'

'Put your reading-glasses on then. Have you got them there?'

'In my pocket.'

'Now take another look,' Priscilla commanded after he had put them on. 'That tiny little rectangle was never caused by accident. No, he's been shaved. Very cleverly too; see how the bare bit blends into his white stripes. The hair's already starting to grow again. We'd probably never have noticed it if he hadn't got quite so wet.'

There she was right. With flattened fur clinging damply to his form, Orestes looked about half his normal size and almost naked.

'Now why, I ask you. It must have happened when you took him back to the surgery. I always said there was something odd about that whole business. And you did too, if you remember. You admitted it.'

George had to allow that he had. 'But he seemed so honest and open when I asked him about it. I can't believe that he . . . Well, assuming that he did, why? What reason could there be?'

'I imagine he wanted to take a blood sample.' Having outlived a number of pet dogs and cats in the course of her career, Priscilla was not inexperienced in such things. 'But why should he want to?' she pondered aloud. 'To see if there's something wrong with him, of course.'

'Yet why should there be?' George protested. 'And if he thought there might be, why keep it a secret from us?'

'That,' said Priscilla grimly, 'is the crux of the matter. And this is where we have it out with him. As soon as possible. What time's the evening surgery, can you remember?'

'You can't go and confront him during his surgery.' George was shocked. 'From all we hear, he's having a rough enough time as it is, and whatever his reasons, I can't really believe that young man's a wrong 'un. Can't we ring up and make an appointment?'

'And give him time to concoct another cover story? No way!' Priscilla was adamant. 'All we need do is arrive there towards the end of the surgery and insist on going in last.'

Our roving reporter's column, which appeared on the nation's breakfast tables, or at any rate altogether too many of them in the opinion of most of Somerstrand's seasonal workers, turned out to be much as Tim had feared.

His mother had been with him that Sunday afternoon, paying one of her frequent visits to make sure that he was 'looking after himself properly', and it was she who had opened the door to the unwelcome caller and ushered him into her son's little sitting-room.

Taken by surprise, Tim had been too tired and harassed by recent events to be diplomatic.

'Where did you get hold of this story?' he had demanded angrily after the man had said his piece, on which he requested Tim's informed comment. Not from the Millers, he was sure, and definitely not the Proctors. 'Certainly not from any reliable source.'

'We have our means,' the reporter returned smoothly.

'Ears at keyholes, I presume.' Tim's wrath was mounting. 'Well, not yours literally, of course not, but that's the origin of the whole thing, I do assure you. And spread by the owner of those over-active ears to a captive audience in a doctor's surgery, where people are usually at their most vulnerable.'

'It wasn't from any of Dr Graylaw's patients that I heard it,' the man persisted, now a shade more conciliatory. 'So if I were to tell you where it came from, would you be prepared to tell me anything about this tropical disease, or whatever it is?'

'No, I wouldn't.' Tim was unmollified. 'You're a journalist, you say. If you already know so much, why don't you have a discussion with the editor of *The Veterinary Record*?'

'Hush, Tim,' Mrs Proud interposed. 'Getting so worked up won't help anyone. Would you like a cup of tea?' she asked their visitor.

'Mother!' Tim exploded.

'Thank you no, Mrs Proud. If your son can't help me, I think I'd better be getting on with the rest of my calls. Mr Cruikshank next, perhaps.'

'Excellent idea!' Tim responded defiantly. 'You know where he lives, I imagine? He's usually in on a Sunday afternoon.'

'Oh dear,' his mother lamented as she closed the door behind the departing figure. 'That was meant to worry you, wasn't it? Is the Crook really so angry with you?'

'Let's say he isn't exactly pleased. And naturally the worse things get, the angrier he'll be. I wouldn't call it reasonable, but one can understand it. At any rate he'll be a damned sight ruder to that little sod than I was.'

'What about Henry Power?' Going into the kitchen, Tim's mother switched on the kettle. 'It's more than likely that man will call on him too, isn't it? Hadn't you better warn him?'

'Yes, you're right.' Tim went swiftly to the telephone, a tactic from which the Colonel evidently profited to the full.

'I gave him a run for his money,' he told Tim, chuckling, the following day. 'Invited him in, gave him a couple of stiff whiskies and waffled on at him for the best part of an hour telling him precisely nothing that he wanted to know. By the end you could see him wondering whether I were really quite sane. And what's more, though he didn't know it, I had my cassette recorder running the whole time behind a curtain. When I played it later I thought it was highly entertaining. You must come round one evening and hear it.'

Such boost as this gave to Tim's morale was inevitably brief. By midday on the Tuesday, by which time there was no longer a copy of the tabloid left unsold in Somerstrand, he was already being made to feel the weight of local displeasure – a chilly nod in the street from the normally over-effusive proprietress of a gift shop, the deliberate avoidance of his eye from the King Charles owner who ran a little café near the harbour, the sight of the tenant of The Black Swan hastily crossing the road to avoid an encounter with him. The one note of cheer, gleaned from Angela as they prepared for evening surgery, was that Marjorie Henshaw was having a pretty rough time too.

'Seems that just now she's even more unpopular than you!' she told him cheerfully.

Now, at nearly six in the evening, the sight of both Bindings minus Orestes sitting wooden-faced on one of the waiting-room benches sent his heart right into his boots. It was all too obvious that they had rumbled him.

'Keep smiling!' Angela managed to mutter to him half mockingly, as she showed out a convalescent labrador plus owner. 'I should have told you. The letter came this afternoon, addressed to you, with "Personal" heavily underlined. He's in the clear; sample negative. Will you come in now, Mr and Mrs Binding?'

'I don't think so, thank you.' George glanced across at the two remaining patients – a small grey kitten and a large white rabbit. 'We'd really rather wait until you've finished.'

'Yes, just as you like.' The brief respite did allow him the chance of a rapid glance at the sheet of paper Angela held out to him some ten minutes later, as the rabbit was borne away. 'Thank God for that. Now it shouldn't be absolutely catastrophic if I have to own up.'

'As from the look of those two I think you're going to have to. So it's a blessing the Crook isn't on duty tonight.'

Not quite so convinced of Tim's duplicity as was Priscilla, George broached the subject with caution.

'It's about Orestes,' he began unnecessarily. 'We've found a surprisingly neat little bare patch on one of his hind legs. No broken skin, no sign of any injury, which puzzles us a little. You wouldn't happen to have noticed it the other evening, I suppose? Or can't you remember? I do realize that you see a large number of animals in the course of a day.'

'Well, not quite so many as usual just at the moment,' Tim answered with a wry smile. 'And yes, I do remember because, to be quite candid with you, I did it.'

'As I thought.'

Priscilla looked grim.

'Um,' said Tim, 'but before you condemn me out of hand I think I'd better tell you a little story. With a happy ending, you'll be glad to hear. Orestes was a stray before you adopted him, wasn't he? You must often have wondered where he came from.'

'Well, naturally,' George answered. 'I even advertised in the local paper.'

'Did you?' his wife exclaimed. 'You never told me!'

'Because I knew you wanted to keep him. On the other hand someone somewhere might have been extremely upset about losing him. Anyway, go on, Mr Proud.'

'Right. Presumably you've read or heard about that newspaper article that came out this morning, the one about Somerstrand? I should think just about everybody has.'

'Oh yes,' they said in unison.

'It sounds as if half the town's gone mad,' George added.

'A lot of people are very upset, but I do think the man who wrote it has gone over the top for the sake of a good story. Nobody at all in the know would give him a scrap of medical information, I gather. I for one refused to. So all he could do was make a great thing of the public reaction here, and as you say, there's certainly been plenty of that.'

'Yes.' Priscilla continued to look severe. 'And so?'

'Well, about eighteen months ago Orestes was brought to me to be put down.'

'But why should anyone have wanted him put down?'

Now she was outraged.

'Because he'd somehow managed to offend the man who owned him. Not an easy character, it seems, and at the moment he's very ill in hospital.'

'Ah,' George said. 'You're talking about that Proctor man whose poodle died or was put down because it was suspected of having the same thing as the Miller dog.'

'That's right, and in the end it turned out that he did have it. In view of everything there had to be a post mortem, you see.'

'So instead of putting the cat down you let him loose. Wasn't there anything else you could have done? He was pretty hungry when he came to us.'

George sounded so disapproving that Tim reddened.

'Still, he's not hungry now, is he? No, I didn't see that there was anything else that I could do. If I'd refused outright, Mr Proctor would simply have taken him to another vet, and Mr Cruikshank would have lost a client. There wasn't anyone else I could think of who would have given him a home, and if I'd taken him to an animal sanctuary I'd have been asked a lot of awkward questions, and at the end of it all he'd probably have been put down there after a few weeks. This way at least he had a chance.'

'I see.' George brought a pipe from his pocket, remembered where he was and put it back. 'I take it Mr Cruikshank knows nothing about this?'

'Lord no, and I beg you never to tell him. He'd be appalled.'

'Yes, he'd think it highly improper,' agreed Priscilla, beginning to sound as if she herself didn't. 'Still, in your place I must admit I'd probably have done the same. So when you realized about the poodle and this Mr Proctor?'

'The poodle, yes. It's not for me to comment about Mr Proctor, but one can draw one's own conclusions.'

'Quite. You thought that since Orestes came from that house he might be incubating the disease, and you'd better try to check up. But could he have been after so long?'

'Well, evidently it's caused by a parasite that can show up almost at once or lie dormant for as long as several years. He couldn't in fact have developed it; it seems cats don't. But they can carry it, we've discovered, so I had to do something in case he was putting you at risk. So I stole a blood sample, if you like, sent it to Bristol for analysis, and was enormously relieved to hear today that the sample was negative.

'And if it hadn't been?'

George was a tougher character than Tim had realized.

'I'd have had to ask you to be tested and explained why. Either way I'm pretty sure you'd have been all right eventually, as you can't have developed any symptoms; it can be treated successfully in the early stages. But we'd all have had to think very seriously about what to do with Orestes.'

'About this illness then,' George wanted to know. 'Is it really such a threat? Is all this panic justified?'

'It's too soon to tell yet.' Tim shrugged rather helplessly. 'It just isn't a thing that crops up naturally in Britain, which is why it took us so long to find out what was wrong with the Miller dog. What we've got to do now is try to trace it to its source, find out how it was brought here. Just one thing, though,' his face clouded over, 'this morning I was forced to put down two apparently healthy dogs because their owners were scared.'

'Oh no!' exclaimed Priscilla. 'That's dreadful.'

'Well, the families had young children, you see, so one can understand it. But I would ask you not to say a word to anyone about the possibility of cats carrying it. If that story gets around we'll have a massacre on our hands.'

Visibly shaken, the Bindings agreed to keep quiet.

'It's a bad business, I must say,' George commented heavily. 'Still, you did what you thought was right and, as to the uproar in the town, it wasn't your fault that your cleaning woman had to go and behave like that. What is it, Priscilla?'

'There's something I just must ask Mr Proud before we go. What was really behind all those antics the other day? When you dragged Orestes and me in through the side door as if the devil were after us and then pushed me out again as if we had the plague? I couldn't work that out at all.'

'Oh that,' Tim said sheepishly. 'You don't know Mrs Proctor, do you? No, you can't do, or I'd have been found out long ago. What happened was that I saw you both outside heading straight for each other and if you'd met she'd almost certainly have recognized Orestes. We had to stop that somehow.'

'We? Who's we? Oh, Angela, I suppose.' To Tim's huge relief she was showing faint signs of amusement as she turned to leave. 'Yes, that I can well imagine.'

'So what's happened?' Angela herself demanded, leaning on her mop as they both watched the Bindings going off down the road. 'She was actually smiling. And she patted me. And what was that she called us – "birds of a feather"?'

23

Jill Graylaw had just put the evening's casserole in the oven when her husband returned home, reasonably sure of a disturbance-free night, as emergency calls for him were being diverted to another doctor.

'Good, you're early,' she greeted him. 'Let's have a drink and then if you like we can watch the six o'clock news before supper.'

'To be honest, I don't think I would, if you don't mind. I've had quite enough news of one kind and another for one day. But I'm all in favour of the drink. Just hang on while I wash my hands.'

'What's happened then?' she asked as he reappeared, and followed him into the sitting-room.

'Oh, it's all this Power-Henshaw-Proctor nightmare.' Going over to the corner cupboard, he mixed them both a gin and tonic. 'Frankly, I'm worried.'

'I can see that.'

'And what's more, so are they at the infectious diseases place.'

'At Bristol, you mean? Where they've got Proctor? So what's happened now?'

'Well, for starters Ivy Miller's blood test showed that she's in the early stages of the same thing. She did come to see me about aching joints a few weeks ago, but aching joints here don't usually indicate tropical disease. Of course at the time I'd no idea about any of this dog business.'

'Is it going to kill her then?'

Jill's glass met the occasional table with a sharp ringing sound.

'With luck not. They're the experts and they think they've caught it in time. But what's worse from the community point of view is that now the damned thing has cropped up somewhere else. The man in charge of Proctor rang me to ask if I could suggest a possible link.'

'And could you? Who else has got it? Where?'

'It's a youngish woman from a village outside Bath. She was lucky in that her GP realized there was something pretty odd wrong with her, and that without benefit of dogs. She's further advanced than Ivy, but even so they reckon she'll survive.'

'But what you're getting at, I presume,' said his wife, 'is that if you can find some connection between her and what's happening here, things won't look too bad. Whereas if it has cropped up elsewhere for no apparent reason, we could be in for trouble. Is that it?'

'In a nutshell. How's your glass?'

'Walter Proctor's firm has a branch in Bath. Thanks.' Jill handed over the empty glass. 'He may well have gone there from time to time.'

'Yes, I've gathered from Ellen that he has.'

'So could he possibly have had an affair with this woman? You did say that it required a certain amount of intimacy to spread the contagion or whatever.'

Graylaw shook his head.

'It's hard to imagine Walter having an affair. I doubt if he could have brought himself to be agreeable for long enough. On the other hand, although she has apparently said that she doesn't know him, she just might be covering up as she's meant to be a respectable married woman.'

'And has he been asked?'

'I think so, but he's too far gone now to make much sense, poor devil. They say it's only a matter of days or even hours.'

'Oh dear,' lamented Jill. 'Poor little Ellen.'

'I'm not sure about that,' her husband said. 'She's still quite young and pretty and I'm sure she's had a hell of a life with him. Ironically she's probably been saved by their recent lack of intimacy, as you so delicately put it. At any rate her sample was negative.'

'That's one blessing. So where do you go from here?'

'I gather that the consultant at Bristol is going to contact the Bath firm about it. The woman doesn't work there, but she could be a client. And then, if it comes to the crunch, I suppose that as a very last resort I'll have to ask Ellen what, if anything, she makes of it.'

24

Telephoned one evening to Clare, the news that the Edenfields were having to postpone their return caused consternation in several quarters.

'I couldn't be sorrier.' Alison had sounded distressed and very guilty. 'But we don't seem to have any choice in the matter. The surgeon here is adamant that Rupert mustn't travel for a few more days and there's also the question of the insurance. He's got to convince some local bureaucrat that he wasn't responsible for the accident, which I'd have thought any fool would realize, but it's obviously better to deal with it on the spot than spend months writing letters from home.' She paused for breath, then plunged. 'Anyway, I hate to ask you, but could you possibly hold the fort for just a little longer? They'll surely have to let us leave some time next week.'

So, seeing no alternative, Clare agreed as pleasantly as she could manage and put the children on to speak.

They too were bitterly disappointed; the novelty of their new routine was wearing off.

'That means we'll have to miss the safari park trip with the cousins,' Anne said crossly. 'And by the way, Clare, Mum forgot to ask you to ring and tell Mr Foster that Dad says there's a file of papers he'll need to collect from here. He'll recognize it when he sees it. It's in Dad's desk; the top drawer.'

Paul was extremely irate about it all.

'It's a bit much, you know,' he grumbled that night, also over the telephone. 'I know it's hard on them, but haven't they anyone else they can call out? I don't see how they can risk running that sort of business without a bit more back-up. What would they have done without you?'

'Alison couldn't have gone, I suppose. But then she was very good to me over Rodsey; not a word of reproach about any trouble all that could have led to here. Still could, I suppose. But that wasn't my fault either. Oh well.' She sighed, glancing at the pile of dirty crocks stacked beside the sink. 'What are you doing tonight?'

'Just watching TV like last night and the one before. Incidentally, there was rather a good film I videoed for you. About a raid on a high street bank. It had five stars, so it seemed worth doing. Lucky for me too, as it happened. The new woman from the flat above came down in the middle of it, asking a whole lot of questions.'

'Nice?' Clare queried, omitting to tell him that she and the children had in fact seen the film.

'So-so. Could be a bit of a clinger. All the more reason for you to reappear on the scene.'

'The moment I can,' she told him.

The worst and most unexpected reaction to the news came next morning from Pam.

'That's awful!' she exclaimed. 'Didn't she mention my day off next Thursday?'

'No, she didn't. Oh dear.'

The system at the kennels was that while each of the kennel maids worked a five-day week, their free days were staggered so that Alison could fill in as required. In the present emergency Clare, assisted by Anne, who was no fool, had done both the previous Saturday and Sunday.

'She's known about it for months. It's my favourite cousin's wedding and it's going to be quite a do. I've simply got to go to it.'

'I suppose Alison forgot.' The implications of this minor bombshell went clicking through Clare's mind. 'Look, I must go now. I'm late for work as it is. But don't worry. We'll think of something.'

'Well, someone will have to.' Clare had never seen her so

worked up. 'I'm sorry to be awkward, but at the end of the day it's not my responsibility.'

At intervals throughout the day Clare racked her brains in an effort to think of somebody who might stand in for Pam, but anyone who occurred to her as a possibility would be bound to be at work. Two retired women who might have obliged were definitely a poor risk. Had she been there, Pam could probably have steered them clear of any potential problem, but certainly not Jane. Clare could scarcely ask Barnet for permission to take a day of her holiday at a time when they were working at full stretch in the absence of old Charters, and should she resort to the dubious line of pretending to be ill, Barnet would be certain to ring up and find her out. At noon her telephone extension rang.

'Mr Charters for you,' Sybil told her.

His voice sounded shaky as he explained what he wanted.

'You'll have heard that Silvestre can't get any more of the leather for the clutch bags with the logo. I'd like to talk to someone there about it. Can you come to do the call this afternoon? You know where I live, don't you?'

'Yes, of course.' Just so long as she was back at the kennels by six o'clock. 'Would about four suit you?'

'That means you'll have to leave around three-thirty,' Barnet said pettishly. 'Why can't any of these people speak English?'

'A lot of them can, but I suppose we've been spoiling them. That's nothing to do with us, though. It was like that when I came.'

Mrs Charters let her in to the little villa on the outskirts of town furthest from the Edenfield establishment.

'He really isn't at all well,' she warned. 'Try to keep him as relaxed as you can.'

One glance at him was enough to show that she was right; his cheeks looked sunken and the pallor of his normally ruddy complexion suggested something rather more serious than a brief indisposition.

'Apart from this hiccup you're managing all right?' he asked her.

'Oh yes,' she said soothingly.

'Barnet will be off to Barcelona soon,' he fretted.

'Yes, but don't worry about that. We'll manage. There's the telephone after all and I can sign letters on your behalf once you've approved them, can't I?'

What with enquiry after enquiry, it was half past four before he would let her put the call through, and when she did the man he wanted was unavailable.

'He'll be working late this evening,' she was told. 'Why don't you try again in another half-hour?'

'Never mind,' said Charters, calmer now. 'My wife will bring us some tea. You don't mind, do you?'

'Er, no,' she lied, 'but in that case would it be all right if I made a call myself? I really ought to be home by six, but it can't be helped.'

'Oh, the kennels. Barnet told me about that. Yes, go ahead.'

Pam sounded even more ruffled than she had expected.

'Oh, honestly!' she exclaimed. 'Jane's already gone. Is there to be no end to this kind of thing?'

'Well, I'm at Mr Charters's house,' Clare said deliberately. 'With him at the moment. If you really need to go on time, I'm sure Anne could cope for twenty minutes or so.'

'Oh no, she couldn't.' There was a hint of rather unpleasant relish in Pam's tone. 'Not this time. You've no idea what's been going on here.'

'What? Tell me.'

'I can't. Not over the telephone.'

'You can give me a hint, surely. Has anyone been hurt?'

'No. We've had an unexpected influx of pugs, but that's only part of it. I'll tell you the rest later. And not too much later, I hope.'

'Not if I can help it,' said Clare.

By the time she eventually made it, crossing a couple of lights on the amber and taking the occasional risk over the speed limit on the quieter roads, it was nearly a quarter to seven.

'I know, I know,' she said before an angrily flushed Pam

could utter. 'I should never, never have given way to the impulse to take this on.'

'Not where other people are involved,' Pam said unkindly. 'And without even having been asked. Still, what's done is done.'

'Sorry.' Clare was abject. 'I've learnt my lesson. But do please tell me what all this is about.'

'Well, this afternoon a Mr Peacock, a solicitor, plainly highly respectable – I've checked on him since – turned up out of the blue with a carload of pugs, three, to be exact. Seems he's an executor of some rich old girl, a Mrs Fanshawe, who died last week. She owned the pugs and left all sorts of instructions in her will as to how they were to be looked after if she died.'

'But not here, surely? Had you ever heard of her?'

'Never.' In her impatience to be off Pam was gabbling at a rate Clare found hard to follow. 'He said someone in his office had suggested this place as an interim home for them. There are some relatives overseas who've inherited the pugs along with her cash, which they only get on condition they do their stuff by them. And it will take them some time to arrange to come over and sort things out.' She reached for her jacket. 'So I've fed them and put them in the big pen next to the Alsatians. Alison's fully booked for the whole of August, so if they're still here then she's going to have problems. Still, that's up to her.'

She headed for the office door.

'Wait, Pam, please, just a moment,' Clare appealed. 'Vaccinations? Their vet?'

'No idea. I suppose you'll have to ring the Peacock man tomorrow from work. That's something I really think is up to you. And oh yes,' she had already opened the door, 'what I didn't want to say over the telephone is that he brought two thousand pounds in cash to keep them going for the moment, which would certainly suggest a fairly long stay.'

'Cash?' Clare echoed. 'As much as that in cash? Why not a cheque?'

'He said it would make it a whole lot simpler for him. She always kept a lot on the premises. So I've locked it in the drawer. You'll have to take it from there.'

But not to the bank, thought Clare, watching her departing figure. No time for that. Still, Alison had a perfectly good safe in the house.

25

Walter Proctor died unaware that he had ever been suspected of having an affair with the woman from Bath, whose name he wouldn't even have known.

'He did meet her, though,' the man from Bristol told Graylaw over the telephone. 'We've cracked it, and it's quite bizarre.'

'Really? Hold on a moment.' Putting the receiver down on his consulting-room desk, he opened the door and gesticulated at Miss Evans, who was surveying some half-dozen patients through her hatch with her customary air of disapproval. 'Turn up the radio, will you, please? As loudly as you dare. I've got Bristol on the line. This is one conversation that simply must not be overheard. Yes?' he said, returning. 'Go on. Tell me.'

'It was on a train. Pretty disgusting really, and rotten luck on her, though she'll make it all right after a long course of treatment. It seems she and her husband were together on this train, nearing Bath, when she decided she had to go to the loo. She ran into Proctor as she was coming out. Diarrhoea, as you'll know by now, is one of the symptoms.'

'So I've discovered.'

'And he must have been having a bout of it in there, as she found out too late. If it weren't so serious, it would be funny. At any rate, to spare you the grisly details, she's a bit short-sighted and she came out in rather a mess and highly distressed.'

'Yes, I can see how that could have happened.' Graylaw had never met the young man, who had only recently joined the

Bristol team, but there was a touch of facetiousness in his manner that grated on his already jangled nerves. It could have been caused by embarrassment, he supposed, trying to be charitable. 'But how can you be certain? You've already told me this woman didn't know Walter Proctor, and in any case couldn't somebody else have had the diarrhoea before he went in?'

'It's a possibility, but we don't think so. The woman said he was looking ill and mopping his brow as he bumped into her and she pointed him out to her husband as they passed Walter's compartment after cleaning her up in another loo.'

'Couldn't the – unpleasantness – have made him look ill?'

'Not for the length of time the mopping-up operation would have taken. He was still looking rotten then, according to the husband. Sporting fellow, that. We're testing him too, of course.'

'Of course. But I still don't see . . .'

'How do we know the man who was ill was Proctor? We know because we got the woman's husband to take a peek at him through the glass door of his ward. He recognized him at once. It seems a bit brutal to have let him see how the disease develops if it isn't tackled in time, but we felt we had no alternative.'

'Quite.' Graylaw sounded unhappy. 'I see that, and I suppose we should all be heartily relieved that you know the source.'

'We know the source of the Bath trouble, yes. But we've still to solve the fundamental part of the mystery – how two of your patients came to be affected. And the answer can only come from you.'

26

Predictably the crowd at Walter's funeral was out of all proportion to his importance in the local community, business or social. In normal circumstances the vicar would have anticipated a turnout of a hundred and fifty or so, but never a church bursting at the seams plus attenders standing crowded together at the back. Out of the corner of one eye he had already registered the presence of a TV van parked discreetly at a short distance from the lych-gate. Now he had to suppress a shudder of distaste as he surveyed the sea of faces before him. A number he recognized as having a genuine reason for being there; the rest were undoubtedly, as an elderly American friend would have put it, rubbernecks.

The cortège was led by a pale and stunned-looking Ellen, flanked by Matthew, who had been called home from his boarding-school. Behind them came a dozen or so relatives and close friends.

Edward Charlton, who liked and had always sympathized with Ellen, and had warned her to expect something like this, had put considerable thought into ensuring that the sensationalists should be disappointed. During his time in Somerstrand he had earned something of a reputation for the cheering and uplifting tone of his funeral addresses, with their little anecdotes about the deceased, their splashes of colour. This one was dryness and dullness personified, brief and bereft of any reference to the cause of Walter's death. All the newshounds learnt, or rather didn't, as they already knew it, was that he had been a local accountant and had left a wife and son. The warm glance this earned him from Ellen showed her complete understanding of his motives.

During the short graveside ceremony there was little he could do personally to protect the family from the attentions of the camera, but ironically it was certain of his less sensitive parishioners who helped there, deliberately obstructing the view in the hope of being seen on the telly.

Afterwards he and his wife, along with a score or so of others, went back to the Proctor house, where two of Ellen's aunts had remained to organize a light tea for them all. Rather to her surprise, Phoebe had been invited too; surprise because it was well over a year since she had had anything to do with Matthew.

'I'm glad you could come.' Ellen broke away from the group surrounding her. 'You were always so supportive with Matthew when things were a bit difficult, and he's never forgotten it, any more than I have.'

Towards the end Phoebe found herself sitting with him on a window-seat. He seemed remarkably little changed, just a couple of inches taller perhaps, and as natural with her as he had always been.

'Will you have to go back to school now?' she asked. 'It must be so very near the end of term.'

'Only to get my stuff,' he told her with an air of obvious relief. 'And I'm not going back next year. Mum says I can come home now and go to Somerstrand Comprehensive.'

How good an idea that was Phoebe was not quite certain, but she realized that Ellen was now likely to be worse off financially than during Walter's lifetime.

'You're pleased about that?'

'Oh yes, very. Most of my real friends are here and I never much liked it there. They're letting Mum off giving a term's notice,' he added, thus seeming to confirm this belief.

'You two look very cosy there,' said the vicar, circulating. 'My two would like you to come and play tennis with them in the holidays, Matthew.'

'Miss Fielding,' Matthew said suddenly after he had gone. 'Would you call me an uncaring person?'

'What?' At the solemnity of his tone it was all she could do not to laugh. 'Why? Has somebody suggested that?'

'Only my housemaster. He thought I wasn't sorry enough about Dad.'

'Oh, really! You mustn't take any notice of that kind of thing. I've known you a whole lot longer than he has and I can tell you here and now that uncaring is the last thing you are. Oh hello, Miss Wood. Shall I get rid of that cup for you?'

He was still sitting there rather forlornly when she returned.

'But you see,' he went on miserably, continuing the conversation as if it had never been interrupted, 'it was true. I wasn't really sorry about Dad. I tried to be, but I couldn't.'

'Maybe, but there's nothing so dreadful about that. I don't think your father was a very happy sort of person and when people are unhappy they aren't always as nice to others as they could be. I know how much you care about your mother.'

'But I didn't really care about Humphrey either.'

Matthew seemed determined to make a full confession.

Phoebe did laugh this time.

'To be honest, I don't imagine anyone did. I do like dogs, but he really was pretty awful, wasn't he?'

'I cared dreadfully about what happened to Marmalade, though. Do you remember?'

'Yes, I do.' At that moment she had to fight down a strong impulse to tell him the truth. It was out of the question, though. It wouldn't have been fair to the Bindings, and goodness only knew what ill effect it might have on Tim's career.

'Matthew,' she said instead, 'since it doesn't upset you too much to talk about your father, you wouldn't have any ideas of your own as to how he and Humphrey and Mrs Miller's dog came to pick up that disease? You do realize it's a foreign one, don't you? Not one you would ever expect to get here. I know a little about it through Tim Proud, you see. It's got everybody baffled.'

'Yes, I know that. None of us had been abroad, though. We always went to Scotland so that Dad could fish.'

'But he or Humphrey could have had some contact with a foreign visitor here,' she pressed him. 'It would have had to be some very physical contact, mind you. Not just a normal conversation or a meal together.' Oh blast, she thought. Across the room one of the aunts was beckoning her. 'Back in a minute,' she said to Matthew. 'Just wait there and see if you can think of anything.'

The aunt was in difficulties over fresh tea supplies.

'Phoebe dear, would you terribly mind going into the kitchen and boiling the kettle? I must pass round the fairy cakes. The sandwiches are all finished.'

'Well?' Phoebe said eventually, returning to the window-seat. 'Any luck?'

'There is one thing I've remembered,' he told her. 'Humphrey did have a pretty horrid fight with a foreign dog. He was bitten quite badly.'

'A foreign dog? Does that mean an Afghan or an Alsatian or whatever, or one that had come from abroad?'

'Come from abroad. He was with a girl who called to see Montse one afternoon. She was on her way home after getting him out of quarantine.'

A tingling feeling ran across Phoebe's scalp.

'Montse? Was she that Spanish *au pair* you had for a while?'

A brief recollection of something Matthew had written in his school diary flashed through her mind, something rather amusing to do with Walter's underclothing.

'That's right. Short for Montserrat. This girl had taught her English when they were both in Spain. Montse was so decent. I wish Dad hadn't sacked her. Mum was very sorry about it too.'

'They can't have been very pleased about Humphrey being bitten by her friend's dog?'

'They never knew. They were both out when the girl came. Come to that, she didn't know either. All we heard at the time was a lot of growling and snapping from out in the garden while we were indoors. Montse and I found the bite later. It was under Humphrey's arm, so we were able to clean it up without the others knowing. There'd have been an awful row about it, you see.'

Phoebe could well believe it.

'Matthew,' she said, 'I think you may just have unearthed something very important. Is there any way of getting in touch with this girl? If her dog infected Humphrey, it could well be doing it to others. Or humans.'

He shook his head.

'I don't know anything about her except that her name was Clare. She had long blonde hair and she seemed nice.'

'But Montse would know how to find her, wouldn't she? Couldn't you write and ask her?'

'No, we've lost touch with her.' He looked more woebegone than ever. 'She sent me a few postcards in the beginning, but Dad wouldn't let me write back.'

'But surely your mother would have her home address somewhere?'

'I don't think so. Not after all this time. She's never been good at keeping letters and things. That used to annoy Dad too.'

Practically everything had seemed to annoy Dad.

'Oh well, never mind, Matthew,' she said. 'In any case we don't want to bother your mother about it now. I've thought of a better idea. Tim will have to contact all the quarantine kennels within a reasonable distance of here. Mr Cruikshank's bound to have a list of them, and there can't be all that many. What did the dog look like? If we don't know Clare's surname, any extra information will help.'

He reflected for a few moments.

'Oh, smallish, brown, with a black muzzle and one of those tails that curl over the back. Rather pretty, really.'

'And his name? Can you remember that?'

He wrinkled his brow.

'Um – I think Montse called him "Seed". But she said it as if it were some kind of joke. I think the girl called him something else, but I don't remember what.'

Not too much help there.

'You can't remember roughly when she came? A year ago?

No, more. Montse's been gone longer than that, hasn't she? You were at school here when she left.'

'Yes, I was. It was summer, I know. We picked some raspberries and had them for tea.'

'Well, we're not doing too badly as detectives, I reckon.' Phoebe rose. 'I'll go and find Tim right now. But if I were you, Matthew, I wouldn't say anything to your mother just yet. All this may have absolutely nothing to do with Clare and until we establish that it has it would be very unkind to give her yet another shock.'

27

'Pam's in a mood,' observed Patrick over the morning cornflakes that Tuesday. 'I've just seen her out in the office.'

'Well, she can't be worrying over Thursday,' Clare responded. 'She's made it very clear that that's my headache. Still, I don't think it would have killed her to ask around about possible stand-ins.'

'She wanted a rise,' Anne put in, 'and they couldn't afford it. Mum says Pam's problem is that she isn't using her qualifications at the moment. She'd earn a lot more somewhere else if she did.'

'And I suppose she feels she has more responsibility just now with your parents away.' Clare glanced at her watch. 'I must have a look at the Yellow Pages. You aren't going to be late for school, are you?'

They didn't think so.

'Why the Yellow Pages?' Patrick asked.

'Just an idea I had in the night. The Jobcentre will never provide a suitable person for one day, especially at such short notice, but a cattery might. Workers at catteries must have days off like everybody else and one of them just might be glad to give one up for the sake of the extra cash. The work here wouldn't be all that different and so long as I avoid a place that takes dogs as well there shouldn't be any rivalry involved.'

There were three fairly local possibilities listed so, making a note of the numbers, she left the house along with the children. The calls she would have to make in her lunch hour from a nearby telephone box. But for once luck was with her.

About mid-morning Barnet took off, saying that he had an urgent matter to discuss with Charters. She allowed ten minutes in case he remembered something and returned unexpectedly, then seized her telephone extension receiver.

It was a case of best of three. The woman answering from the first cattery seemed to think it an extraordinary request and that Clare must be slightly insane. At the second place a man answered and said no, he was sorry but he had nobody who could be available to do what she asked. At the third she struck oil, after a long pause while the girl at the other end consulted rotas and then went off in search of the prospective candidate, who eventually agreed after asking what she would be paid.

'I don't know,' was all Clare could say. 'Certainly the going rate, whatever that is, plus a bit more to make up for the favour you'd be doing us. I know Mrs Edenfield will be fair about that.'

That settled it.

'If you can come at half past eight I'd be very glad,' she added. 'You won't see me for more than a moment because I have to be off to work elsewhere, but I'll write everything down for you and there'll be another girl called Jane who'll help you.'

So, greatly relieved and anticipating a peaceful if unexciting evening, she arrived back at the kennels in time to relieve the two helpers at six o'clock.

'How's it gone?' she asked Jane, who was fiddling somewhat half-heartedly round the office with a broom. 'Pugs settling in all right.? Any developments?' The other girl, it struck her, was looking thoroughly under the weather, hair dishevelled and dark circles beneath her eyes.

'No, nothing. They seem all right.'

Whether or not she intended the slight emphasis on the 'they' was anyone's guess.

'That's good. I expect they've been having a pretty poor time lately, with everything revolving round a sick old lady.'

'Mrs Baxter's collected Timmy, and there are two new day-dogs starting tomorrow. And three boarders for ten days from

Monday. You can see it all in the book; Pam filled it in. I've sold a couple of leads too.' She glanced up at the cluster of leather thongs dangling from a hook in the ceiling. 'Pam's gone.' This with a hint of malice.

'Oh, said Clare, not rising. 'Well, I suppose I owed her that after last night. So you'll be off now. Out with Harold?'

Jane shook her head.

'Not tonight. He was back for thirty-six hours on Sunday, but he left for Spain again this morning.'

She looked so wretched that Clare couldn't help feeling a pang of sympathy.

'Poor Jane. Never mind; perhaps he'll bring you back something nice.'

'That'll be the day.' Jane shook her hair out over her jacket collar. 'Well, I'll be going.'

'And try to have a peaceful evening,' Clare advised. 'You look a bit part-worn, to put it mildly. See you tomorrow.' Opening the door that connected the office with the house, she called to the children, whose voices she could hear upstairs, 'I'm back! You two OK? Had your tea?'

'Hi, Clare!' Anne came to the top of the stairs. 'Yes. Just going to get our so-and-so homework out of the way and then we're watching TV. It's good tonight. You'll be up soon, won't you?'

'Soon as I can.' Returning to the office, she cast an eye over the registration book, which confirmed what Jane had told her. There was a note from Pam to the effect that Peacock had telephoned to enquire after the pugs and had managed to supply the required information as to vaccinations – a note that proved Pam's intention of recouping what she could of her involuntary overtime the previous evening. In the desk drawer she found Mrs Baxter's cheque and the money for the dog leads.

So that was that for the day. Thankfully she locked the outside door and from sheer force of habit, the front door of her own flat being glass-paned, slipped the key into her pocket, then turned to go into the house proper.

What happened next was totally shocking, giving her a

fright she would never quite forget. On the outer side of the office was the fair-sized all-purpose washroom where the dog-dishes were dealt with in a sink next to the basin intended for human use. At the far end was a tall, narrow cupboard. As she watched in sheer disbelief, its door opened and a tall figure in jeans, its face covered by a balaclava, emerged with a gun, or what looked like one, in its hand.

'Right,' it said softly. 'Now we don't want any fuss, do we? The kids are upstairs. There's no one else around. You're just going to take me quietly to the safe, wherever it is, and hand over the cash.'

'Cash?' Clare quavered.

'You heard. Don't come the little innocent with me. All that lolly you put in it yesterday. Come on,' he urged, agitating his weapon as she blinked at him in stupefaction. 'Their insurance will probably cover it and you wouldn't like the kids to get hurt, would you? Or yourself, come to that.' There was a pause. 'Go on. Move!'

Clare gasped, then some kind of inner mechanism seemed to take over, numbing all emotion. In what amounted to a state of shock she realized that she had no alternative but to lead the way into the house, straight into the rarely used and orderly sitting-room. Over to the right was the kitchen door, left closed by the children after they had helped themselves to their meal.

As she already knew, they were upstairs in the family living-room. She could hear their voices but not yet of course the television sounds that would have reassured her as to the likelihood of their staying there.

The safe was in a small utility room next door to them. She walked softly upstairs, closely followed by the predator, found the key, unlocked it and, with a shaming sense of defeat, handed over the thick manilla envelope containing the notes.

'Not much else, is there?' he said nastily, peering in. 'I'll leave you the rest for the housekeeping.'

'Too kind of you,' she managed to murmur, cautiously opening the door to the landing and always conscious of his presence behind.

At that moment, to her horror, Patrick emerged.

'Clare, I'm stuck with my French. Old Potter never explains anything properly. Can you?'

She glanced back over her shoulder, thankful that she couldn't see the expression beneath the balaclava.

'I'll try. Can you get on with something else for just a few minutes?'

'OK.'

Suspecting nothing, he went back in and shut the door.

Once downstairs, 'Now will you get out!' she demanded, anger rising as physical safety seemed to be becoming more assured.

'You surely didn't think I was planning a social evening with you?'

His soft laugh was singularly unpleasant.

'Better go through the front then.'

That was when the doorbell rang and, startled, with a final threatening movement of his weapon, he hastened back through the sitting-room and out into the office. There he would be frustrated, she realized with thumping heart; the key to the now locked door was in her pocket. If only he had chosen the kitchen, which led to the back door.

But there on the front step stood Bill Foster, come to collect the papers from Rupert's desk.

'Oh, hello! I'm afraid I can't ask you in just now,' she told him, her tone almost shrill.

'No?' He looked distressingly taken aback. 'Well, I've come from the far end of town and I really must pick up Rupert's papers. I shan't keep you a moment.'

'It's not that. I wasn't doing anything,' she said lamely, and stood rigid as, with an air of faint bewilderment he walked past her and into the sitting-room, which he obviously knew. The gunman was nowhere to be seen, but the familiar sound of a closing door told her that, unable to make his escape to the outside world, he must have taken refuge in his second cupboard of the evening, a deep walk-in one beside the hearth. He would find it dark and airless, she thought with satisfaction; lucky for him that there wasn't a key in the hole.

'How's it going?' Foster asked, looking at her as though scenting trouble. 'You seem a bit peaky and uptight. Finding it a strain?'

'Not really. There've been a few problems, but I think we've sorted them. Look, I'm sorry about just now. It wasn't that I wasn't pleased to see you. Will you have a drink?'

She prayed that he wouldn't opt for coffee, which would involve her taking a trip to the kitchen. It was hard to be sure how much the intruder could hear, but should anything lead him to suspect her of slipping off to fetch help he might well come bursting out and Foster struck her as being the kind of person to put up a fight. In fact it was all right.

'That would be nice,' he said. 'They keep the drink in the cabinet. Maybe I'll help myself to a beer. What about you?'

Relieved that there were glasses there too, Clare just managed a smile and sat down rather shakily.

'Actually I rather wanted to talk to you,' he went on, returning, glass in hand, to his chair. 'I gather you aren't too happy in your present job.'

'It isn't the job exactly,' she replied, wondering how she could ever succeed in keeping up a rational conversation, while aware that this one might well be important for her. 'I've always liked the work. It's just that the new manager is doing his best to get my job for his girlfriend, and he's making things as difficult for me as he can. I hate being beaten, but there does come a time . . .'

'Quite. That's nasty. Well, I don't know if you know anything about it, but I hear on the import-export grapevine that your Mr Charters is going to retire for health reasons.'

'Is he?' She was shocked. 'I suppose I should have thought of that. He looked awful when I saw him yesterday. But . . .'

The telephone rang. It was Paul, as she had desperately hoped, for even as she talked to Foster one part of her brain had been hatching up a possible way of saving the day, but to make it work needed him and only him.

'Paul,' she said deliberately, 'I'm glad you rang. I'm afraid I really can't make it to that film tonight.'

'What film? I don't get you.'

'No, I'm sorry. I'm being held up, you see. An unexpected caller.' Out of the corner of one eye she could see from Foster's expression that any chances of the job it had seemed he might offer her were definitely receding.

'You surely don't mean a burglar?'

'That's right.'

'Then I'll ring the police straight away.'

'Yes, do. After all, the film will be on for several days.'

'I'm sorry I've wrecked your evening,' Foster said coldly as she replaced the receiver. 'You should have told me. I'll just collect my papers and be off.'

There was no way she could actually ask him to stay. If he could hear, as he almost certainly could, she had now decided, the man in the cupboard could hardly fail to put two and two together.

'You haven't wrecked my evening,' was all she dared say. 'My friend and I can just as easily go out another night.'

It was then that Foster's expression suddenly changed. She turned her head, following his glance, to see that the cupboard had opened just a fraction of an inch; the air in there must have been getting short. He had presumably seen it happen, possibly even the handle move; nothing less could account for the shock in his eyes when they met hers. Her position, back towards the hiding place, permitted her to nod slightly in confirmation and place a wary finger to her lips.

'The papers you want are in the desk drawer, aren't they? I'm afraid I may have buried them under all the letters that have come for Rupert and Alison. Shall I help you look?'

'Yes, thanks. If you pick the top ones out I'll dig underneath. You wouldn't recognize the ones I want; they're all to do with the business.'

Standing up, he went over and opened the drawer. There were of course no letters, but between them they put up a quite convincing show of turning over papers. While she could sense the furious activity of Foster's brain, Clare's main concern was not to try the gunman's patience too far. How long would the police take? Ten minutes? A quarter of an hour?

'I think these may be what you want,' she said at length, holding out the first sheets that came to hand. 'I'm sorry about the muddle. I should have been a bit more careful.'

'M'm. Let's see. Yes, these are what I wanted. There should be one more, though.' Aware now of what she was trying to do, he rummaged again. 'Right, that's it. I'd better be off, but first I think I'd better just go up and say hello to the kids. I always do when I come here.'

'Of course. I'm sure they'd be furious if you didn't. I'll come too.'

Together they made their escape. They had hardly reached the landing when Clare heard the front door slam.

'Thank Heaven! He's gone. I just hope not too soon.'

Followed by Foster, she rushed into the utility room, where the safe still stood open, and over to the window. Outside it was still broad daylight, not a soul in sight, the occupants of the neighbouring houses presumably either eating or glued to their television sets. Every car to be seen was sedately parked in its owner's drive.

'Looks as though he's got away,' she said, turning back with the utmost depression. 'And we tried so hard, didn't we? Oh, hell!' And as Foster patted her shoulder, 'No, I'm not going to cry. Blast him, the rotten brute!'

'What is it, Clare?' Startled by her upraised voice, the children came out onto the landing. 'What's happened? Why's the safe open? Hello, Mr Foster,' they added as a polite afterthought.

'Well, we've been burgled. A man with a gun or what passed as one made me hand over the two thousand pounds that came in yesterday. Oh, what a homecoming for your parents!'

'But how did he get in?' Anne demanded. 'We didn't hear anything. Just that ring at the door. Was that him?'

'That was me,' Foster said. 'And I don't know anything either, just what happened at the very end. Should we all go down and have a cup of tea or something while you tell us, Clare?'

Her narrative had hardly got under way before it was

interrupted by another ring at the door and a yell of 'Clare! Are you all right?'

Flushed and agitated, Paul had plainly gone through it at second-hand.

'Come in,' she said. 'We're all in the kitchen. Yes, we're fine, but I'm afraid he's got away with an awful lot of money.'

'Oh, but he didn't!' Now Paul was triumphant. 'No, the police managed to set up roadblocks a little way down the road in either direction. Too far away for you to hear the rumpus. When he saw them he jumped out of his car – stolen, incidentally – and tried to make a run for it, but he hadn't a chance. They were very suspicious of me,' he added, grinning. 'It took me quite a time to convince them that it was I who made the 999 call. Anyway, they'll be sending along someone to talk to you within the next hour or so.'

'So we'll get the money back,' Patrick said with relief.

'Yes, you will.'

'I was a bit slow on the uptake, wasn't I?' said Foster after he and Paul had been introduced. 'I did think you were behaving rather oddly, but it never occurred to me that of course "held up" had two meanings.'

'You probably didn't see that BBC2 film last week. What was it?'

'Cash on Demand,' the children said in unison.

'So you'd already seen it when I told you I'd videoed it for you.' Paul looked slightly hurt. 'Why didn't you say so?'

'Wouldn't it have been rather unkind when you'd gone to that trouble? Anyway, what a good thing you did! Now we can keep it for posterity. And put it on for Rupert and Alison. They'll be thrilled to bits.'

'It was a nasty moment when I saw the cupboard door move,' Foster reminisced. 'Very little, but twice; there wasn't any doubt about it.'

'It was very lucky that you did. Otherwise you'd have left in high dudgeon and the police would never have made it in time.' She thought it politic not to tell Patrick how near he had been to coming face to face with the robber. It was a story that would no doubt have impressed his schoolmates, but might boomerang by making him nervous later on.

Detective Sergeant Robinson, who arrived a little later, was a tall man verging on middle-age with shrewd pale blue eyes and a bald dome of a head. He nodded at the little group and sat down, refusing the offer of a drink.

'Now let's hear all about it. Mr Eddison here tells me he dialled 999 after what you might call a coded message from a Miss Forrester. That you, miss?'

'Yes. And this is Mr Foster, Mr Edenfield's employer. He walked in right in the middle, came to collect some papers, but he didn't actually see the burglar.'

The two men nodded to each other.

'Right,' Robinson said. 'So put me in the picture, will you. Tell me the whole story in your own words.' As if she could have told it in anyone else's, thought Clare. 'And don't hurry; take your time.'

'Very well. I came in from work via the office, as I've been doing each day, checked the records left by one of the two kennel maids, locked the outer door and put the key in my pocket and was about to go through the communicating one into the house when this man appeared out of the washroom brandishing what looked like a gun, and forced me to let him through.'

'He had two thousand pounds in notes on him when he was caught. I take it that was what he was after?'

'Yes, no question. He'd obviously found out somehow that there was an unusually large sum of money in the safe.'

'M'm.' The policeman drummed thoughtfully on the table with the fingers of one hand. 'And did you recognize him?'

'Not a chance. His face, apart from the eyes, was covered by a balaclava.'

'Not even his voice?'

'I'm afraid not. I don't actually work here, you see. I'm just a friend standing in because Mr Edenfield, these children's father, had an accident in France and his wife was desperate to get over to him.'

'M'm,' the detective sergeant repeated, thrusting his chin

up and down as if this in some way aided his thought processes. 'And how do you imagine he got into the washroom without being seen?'

'Easily enough, I should think. The office is always unlocked during the day and the girls are often out of sight down the paddock. Customers just go in and ring the bell. He would only have needed to watch for the right moment and then walk in and hide in the broom cupboard in case somebody should come in for a wash. If he'd been interrupted he could have said he'd come to buy a dog lead. They do sell a few and nobody seems interested in stealing them.' She paused, then asked nervously, 'Was it a real gun?'

'Real and loaded,' he said grimly. 'Now about this cash. Have you any idea how he could have come to know about it?'

'I can't imagine. It came yesterday, quite out of the blue as an advance payment for boarding three dogs whose owner had died. What's more, he knew it was yesterday. He said so.'

'So someone from the owner's household could have known?'

'I don't know. It was an executor, a solicitor, who came here. But the man must have realized that the Edenfields wouldn't be here. He said, "The kids are upstairs and there's nobody else around." Or something like that.'

'I see.' There was another pause during which the chin continued its movements. 'What about other customers then? Would anyone else have witnessed the transaction over the dogs?'

'That's something I'd have to ask Pam. She's the older girl who actually dealt with it. But I can't see a solicitor doing a thing like that in public, can you? Wouldn't he have waited till Pam and he were alone?'

'One would think so,' Robinson agreed. 'This man then. We know him; he's a petty crook, name of Clitheroe, with a string of minor convictions. This would be the first time we've heard of him carrying a gun, so maybe you had a lucky escape. What is it, sir?'

Foster had let out a startled exclamation.

'Probably nothing. There's a man on my payroll, an HGV driver called Clitheroe, but it isn't all that uncommon a name and, quite apart from the fact that I would surely know if he had any kind of criminal record, he couldn't have done it himself because he's in Spain at the moment on a job for me.'

And as Robinson shrugged, dismissing the remark with the contempt he clearly thought such an irrelevance deserved, Foster persisted, with a hint of annoyance. 'I merely mentioned it because, as you won't know, or wouldn't have until a few minutes ago, Mr Edenfield also works for me, although his status in the firm is very different. They wouldn't socialize, but they do know each other.'

'What's more,' nettled, Clare went to his defence, 'one of the two kennel maids here is Harold Clitheroe's girlfriend. She knew about the money and I bet you anything she saw him last night, since he was going off this morning. I'm not for a moment suggesting that she'd be a party to anything criminal, but it's more than likely that she told him about it in all innocence. And couldn't your Clitheroe be a brother or cousin or something?'

Too late she remembered the affair of the smuggled pup. Jane had undeniably been an accessory after that particular fact and if it were to come out now, much the same would go for Alison. Maybe she should have left Foster to fight his own battles.

As it was, the result was an acknowledgement from Robinson that the two of them might well after all have a point.

'We'll check it out and see if there is any connection. We've got our man, which is the main thing – his first name is Brian, by the way – but we could make things pretty hot for your Harold too if we found that he had been passing on information of that nature to a known criminal.'

'And Jane?' Clare asked nervously.

'Much more difficult. As you plainly realize, she could claim complete innocence of any criminal intent, and possibly genuinely at that. So what I suggest is that you all go about your early morning routine as if nothing unusual had happened and don't say a word to anyone. If this Jane is in on it, that's bound to rattle her and she may let something slip.'

'If she's in on it, won't she be wondering how the second Clitheroe got on?' Paul wondered. 'Or could she possibly find out tonight?'

'That's anyone's guess. She certainly could tomorrow, as he'll have the right to see a solicitor. But don't let's speculate too much; our man may still be someone entirely different. And I'd be grateful if the three of you could come down to the station to make statements. Say about ten o'clock? Not convenient?'

He had caught Clare's look of dismay.

'It's only that things are terribly busy at the office just now. Still, I suppose it can't be helped.'

'Of course it can't,' said Foster with considerable warmth. 'And I shouldn't worry about it if I were you. You're only too welcome to start working for me any time, and on terms and conditions at least as good as your present ones. We can discuss it whenever you like. Not tonight, though. My wife will be wondering what in the world has happened to me.'

'Mine's used to it,' remarked Robinson rather gloomily as he too rose to go. 'You'll be all right, though, will you?' he asked Clare. 'It must have been quite a shock. You won't be nervous? No need to be now we've caught him.'

'Still, I think it mightn't be a bad idea if I stayed,' Paul suggested.'What do you think, kids? There must be a sofa somewhere that I can use.'

'Oh, there is.' Relief was written all over Anne's face. 'In the living-room upstairs. Quite comfortable, really. I'll get you some blankets and a pillow.'

'Great,' Paul agreed. 'Just so long as you don't make me too comfortable, because I've got to get myself and the car well clear of the place before the kennel maids show up tomorrow.'

Ten minutes later the telephone rang.

'Shall I?' Clare asked Patrick, who was still hovering around, too excited and overwrought to go to bed.

Upstairs his sister was having difficulty in locating blankets, to judge from the sounds of drawers being opened and shut and the familiar creaking of the linen cupboard door.

It was a surprise to hear Alison's voice. By now in France it would be well after eleven o'clock.

'Clare? Hope I'm not catching you at an awkward time. I just wanted to let you know that we're leaving tomorrow and should be home some time on Saturday evening. I'm not sure about train times, but we'll take a taxi from the station. Only another two days, thank Heaven. Is everything all right your end?'

'Oh yes. Would you like to speak to the children?'

'Only if anyone's there.'

'Patrick is.'

She handed him the receiver.

'Hi, Mum. Are you really coming home? Is Dad OK?' There was a quaver in his voice that his mother could scarcely miss. 'No, everything's all right.' He had caught the warning glance. 'Would you like to say goodbye to Clare?'

'Are you certain there's nothing wrong? Patrick did sound odd. You're not hiding anything, are you?'

Clare took a deep breath.

'No, of course we're not. He's a bit puffed, that's all. He's been playing some wild game in the garden, and Anne's just gone up to have first bath. Anyway, be careful on the journey. I hope it won't be too difficult for you. But everything here's fine.'

28

Phoebe's news, which she imparted to Tim with a sense of real achievement, was rather disappointingly received.

'It could well be a breakthrough,' he agreed, 'and certainly worth following up, but there's no way we can tackle all the quarantine places. The Crook's list runs into several pages of close type and we can't take it for granted the Spanish dog was left near here. This Clare girl could have picked him up from practically anywhere in the south of England and spent a night somewhere on the way to visit Montse.'

'She could.' Phoebe scowled at him. 'But that would indicate a pretty strong friendship, wouldn't it? Somerstrand's very much out on a limb, after all; not really on the way to anywhere. Surely it's more likely that the dog was in, say, Devon or Dorset? In any case, what alternative have we?'

'Another go at the Proctors, I should say.'

Wandering into his little kitchen, Tim eyed a wilting lettuce with suspicion.

'Would this do for a salad, do you think, or not?'

'Do,' she said shortly. 'I'll strip it. But how do you reckon you can get any more out of the Proctors? And at a time like this, to boot?'

'Time like this my foot!' he said infuriatingly. 'Ellen Proctor's life's been drastically changed, of course it has, but don't let's kid ourselves that she's heartbroken. Everything you've ever told me about that family, and you've told me quite a lot, if you remember, has shown that he must have been hell to live with. We'll go about it very delicately, I promise. Tomorrow afternoon, say? After school?'

'All right, if you say so.' She shrugged. 'She just might be able to think of some way of tracking down Montse's address, I suppose, but how you think you can make Matthew remember more than he says he does I can't imagine. You're not a hypnotist. And what's more, he may already have gone back to school. He told me that he had to, to pick up his stuff.'

As it happened, Matthew was still at home when, after first warning Ellen by telephone, Tim and Phoebe arrived.

'I had to tell Mum what I thought you must be trying to find out,' he said, 'because of Mr Proud coming too, you see.'

They did.

'I hope it didn't upset her too much,' Phoebe said nervously.

'I don't think so.' The boy led the way into the sitting-room. 'I'll fetch her. I think it's business things that are worrying her mainly.'

Ellen did indeed look rather distraught.

'Hello, dear,' she greeted Phoebe. 'Hello, Mr Proud.'

'Tim.'

'Yes, well, Tim. It's nice to see you both and get away from all the horrible papers. Lots of letters to answer; I can do them in due course, but I do wish Walter had explained a bit more about the business side of things – rates and income tax and car licences and pension contributions, you know. It's not that he wasn't methodical. It's all there, but he didn't tell me anything very much. Well, naturally he had no idea that he would die so soon.'

She sighed.

'I'm sure there'll be lots of people to help you,' Tim encouraged her. 'His solicitor, people in the firm and so on. If he's been methodical it shouldn't be too difficult.'

'Well, I hope you're right.' She didn't seem too convinced. 'Anyway, to change the subject, Matthew has told me about the girl who came here with her dog. Till you rang I hadn't heard a thing about it.' She looked at her son, who wriggled uncomfortably and stared down at the floor. 'Still, I do understand why. So how can I help?'

'Well, for everyone's sake I think we should try to find this girl and discover if she has had any experiences like yours. For one thing, if we definitely knew that it was she, or rather her dog, who brought the disease to the town, the locals might calm down a bit and stop sniping at each other. And if the dog is still carrying the parasite without her knowledge it should be tested, and steps taken to prevent a similar outbreak somewhere else.'

'Oh dear,' Ellen said. 'Provided it isn't already too late. I think I'd better get us all some coffee.' Going into the kitchen she called back, 'But what can I do? If Matthew can't help, I don't see how I can.'

'You must surely have some information about this Montse tucked away somewhere. Old letters, correspondence arranging for her to come to you. You know the kind of thing. Because she's more than likely to know how we can find Clare.'

'I suppose so.' Reaching for a jar of instant coffee, Ellen spooned some of the contents into each of four mugs. 'But I really haven't you know. Matthew and I liked Montse, in fact he was very attached to her and the way she left was really quite distressing. She did send him a few postcards, but never one with an address on and Walter would certainly have destroyed all the earlier correspondence.'

'But how did you get her in the first place?'

'Through some agency in London, I think, but I don't remember its name, in fact I don't think I ever knew it. Walter organized it all, you see, as he always did.'

At which point, accepting their mugs, Phoebe and Tim acknowledged defeat.

'Then Matthew's our last hope, I think,' Tim said. 'I know he's told Phoebe all he can, or all he thinks he can, but we just might be able to get him to remember something more. Would you mind, Matthew?'

Matthew didn't, but his expression was sceptical.

'Will this worry you, Mrs Proctor?' Phoebe asked gently.

'Not in the least,' she answered, looking rather brighter. 'In fact I'll be quite interested. Is it all right if I stay?'

'Well, of course.'

'Now look, Matthew,' Tim began, 'have you ever been back to a place you'd almost forgotten? Somewhere you couldn't describe accurately to anyone else. And yet when you're there again after a long time and come to a certain part of it, say a road, you suddenly remember exactly what's going to be round the next corner?'

'No.'

Matthew shook his head and Tim had the uneasy feeling that he was beginning to weary of the whole procedure.

'Oh, but I have!' his mother exclaimed. 'Quite often. It's only that you're young, darling, and haven't been around a great deal.'

'Exactly.' Tim smiled gratefully at her. 'Sorry about badgering you, Matthew, but if we can't get Montse to find Clare for us, we might well get Clare to find Montse.' A point which registered, he noticed. 'Anyway, it's worth a try, don't you think?'

Matthew supposed it was.

'So you and Humphrey were alone in the house when this girl Clare arrived with her dog. Was Montse expecting her, do you think?'

'I don't know, but they did seem awfully pleased to see each other.'

'Can you remember what language they spoke? English or Spanish?'

Matthew wrinkled his brow.

'A bit of both, I think. English to me, of course.'

'So did you stay with them all the time Clare was here?'

'Oh no.' He was quite shocked at the suggestion. 'I knew they wanted to talk on their own, so I went out into the garden with Humphrey and picked some raspberries for tea.'

'And where was the Spanish dog then?'

'Indoors with them until they decided to let him out for a run. I must have come in then. Yes, that would be how he and

Humphrey came to have the fight. None of us saw it, just heard it.'

At this point he looked so guiltily at his mother that Phoebe felt sorry for him. Still, how could he have anticipated that leaving the two dogs outside on their own would have such disastrous consequences? Assuming, of course, that it had.

'You're doing extremely well, you know,' Tim encouraged him. 'Were they pleased with the raspberries?'

'Yes, I think so. And I looked in the cupboard for a tin of cream.'

'Lovely.'

At that point Phoebe decided to take over.

'And that is presumably when Clare did most of her talking to you. Over the raspberries. Try to picture yourself passing the sugar and so on. I know how welcome you'd have made her feel. Did she tell you how the dog reacted when he saw her that morning? It was that morning, I suppose?'

'I think so. She said he went absolutely mad and leapt all over the place, but when he got outside he seemed a bit strange until he was put in the car. There was some trouble about finding his travelling box among the others in the hut where they were stored. She had that on her roof-rack. I saw it. It was enormous, with holes in and green labels.'

Trying to conceal her growing excitement, Phoebe glanced at Ellen for permission and passed the boy a plate of shortbread.

'You said "when he got outside" and that boxes were kept in a hut. Did she mention anything else about the outside? Anything she thought might amuse you, I mean. Otherwise I doubt if she'd have bothered.'

'I don't think so.' Matthew began to nibble. 'Oh yes, it's coming back now. There was a pig in an open pen. An enormous one, she said.'

'A pig?' Tim echoed. 'You're not suggesting there was a pig in quarantine?'

'No, no.' The boy actually laughed, 'Just a visiting pig. Called Llewellyn. Clare thought that was rather funny.'

'It must have been a Welsh pig,' commented Ellen, almost

smiling. 'Now why would one have a visiting pig?'

'Presumably because one has a resident sow.' Tim smiled back at her. 'With a name like Llewellyn the pig would have to be a boar. Which suggests a farm. Did she say it was a farm, Matthew?'

'No, she didn't. Or if she did I don't remember.'

'All the same I think it probably was. Where's that list, Phoebe? Thanks.'

'This is the list of registered places the Ministry of Agriculture, Fisheries and Food sends out to people who are going to have to quarantine pets coming in from abroad,' he explained to Ellen. 'Clare's dog must have been in one of them, but it would be an appalling performance to have to ask them all. So what we've been hoping is that Matthew might manage to narrow it down for us, and I rather think he has.'

'Have I?' he asked hopefully. 'It didn't seem much good yesterday. Today is better.'

'Well, yesterday must have been really tough for you both,' Tim sympathized. 'I suppose Clare didn't mention the name of whoever runs what we hope is this farm?'

'She might have done. Yes, I think perhaps she might. To Montse, not to me. Mrs Something-or-other. But I never could remember it – not in a thousand years.'

'Doesn't matter. Now let's look, Phoebe. It's done in areas. Let's see if we can find anywhere with "farm" in the name within sixty to eighty miles or so from here. Do you mind, Mrs Proctor? Because we do rather need Matthew a little longer.'

'Of course I don't. Actually there are a couple of telephone calls I ought to make. I can do them while you're searching. And do finish the shortbread. You'll be needing it before you're through.'

Rather to the relief of both Phoebe and Tim, she took herself off to the hall.

'And before we start,' Tim warned Phoebe rather fiercely, 'if you should find a farm, don't mention either its or the owner's name out loud.'

'What do you take me for?' she demanded indignantly. 'D'you think I don't see what you're up to? And for the same reason don't you look over anyone's shoulder, Matthew.'

'I won't.' With a ghost of a smile the boy stretched out a hand towards the plate. 'And don't think I don't see either.'

Tim was suitably chastened.

Within two minutes they had found three possibilities within the limits they had set themselves – Underdown Farm, some sixty miles away, Hampton Farm, around eighty and there was also Cloverdene Farm, a regrettable hundred and fifty.

'Right,' said Tim. 'Could you find a piece of paper, Matthew?' And turning his back so that the boy was unable to see which names he wrote immediately and which required a few seconds' thought, he compiled a list of twenty. 'Now I know you can't remember the name Clare mentioned, but you may be able to pick it out from the ones on this list. It's what's called passive knowledge. Take a look.'

He and Phoebe held their breath while Matthew did so, frowning and running his eye a good half-dozen times up and down the list. Any recognition he might claim looked unlikely to be exactly spontaneous.

'Yes,' he said at last. 'Mrs Vinicombe. Definitely Mrs Vinicombe.'

'Absolutely certain?'

'Yes. Clare mentioned her when she was helping Montse with the washing-up.'

'That's wonderful, Matthew!' Phoebe exclaimed in delight. 'You've done it! Underdown Farm!'

29

Tim was astonished by the Crook's reaction to the little detective story which he related to him next morning. Gone was his habitual gruffness of manner, in fact he was positively gracious.

'I call that most ingenious of you both,' he said, beaming. 'Extremely enterprising. A word of warning, though. The boy could have been wrong about the name. He might have heard it somewhere else, seen it on a shopfront or anything. Still, we can but hope.'

'We do realize that,' Tim agreed. 'It's very much a shot in the dark.'

'The other thing,' the Crook pursued, 'is that the people who run this place, should you find them, may well refuse to give you the girl's address. Confidentiality, you know. I really think the best and quickest thing you can do is drive over there and see them, taking all your credentials and a note from me to back you up. The fact that you're a vet should help. Failing that, you could ask them to send a letter to her, provided they can work out who she must be. Yes, that's probably the answer. Why don't you go tomorrow and take your Phoebe with you? She won't be working on a Saturday and I can manage here on my own.'

Tim could hardly suppress a gasp. This was almost too good to be true. What in the world could have come over his boss? Gradually all became clear.

'Your Phoebe.' The older man cleared his throat. 'Nice girl. Pretty too. Very good the way she handled that boy and obviously they think a lot of her at the school. Er – you are going to marry her, I take it? I mean to say, you've been going about together a long time. Don't you think . . ?'

Tim burst out laughing.

'Oh yes, we're getting married once we're sure I'm going to be able to make a go of this job, but we do realize this last drama can't have done the practice much good. It's not a question of my making an honest woman of her, if that's what you're thinking. We're both a bit old-fashioned, I suppose.'

'Oh, quite, quite, quite!' The Crook embarrassed was a highly entertaining sight. 'No, it's just that I have a little proposition to put to you. If you've a minute or two to spare, can you come into the inner room to discuss it?'

Wondering what on earth was coming next, Tim followed him.

Phoebe was delighted at the prospect of a trip to Underdown Farm. It was a bright, sparkly, breezy day, and Tim had taken the trouble to work out the quietest route, avoiding major roads as far as possible. For their picnic lunch he backed the car up a rutty lane that smelt pleasantly of cattle and clover.

'There's something on your mind,' Phoebe accused as she filled their mugs with tea from a Thermos and handed him a Cornish pasty. 'Tell me.'

'I'd rather not quite yet. You'll see why when I do. Oh, it's nothing at all to worry about, in fact it could be something quite nice. Don't let it spoil the day for you.'

'No,' she said doubtfully. 'All right.'

Even so, she could hardly help casting him an anxious glance from time to time.

Underdown Farm was an L-shaped white building approached by what in winter would be a very muddy lane. The field beside it was quite densely populated with sheep and from one outbuilding came the reassuring grunt of pigs.

'If it's the quarantine kennels you're wanting,' an overalled man on a tractor told Tim when asked, 'they're in the building over there, right on up the lane.'

Immediately outside the noise of barking coming from the runs beyond was deafening. A girl in green dungarees, armed with a mop and bucket, looked enquiringly at them.

'We're trying to discover the whereabouts of a young lady whose dog was here,' Tim ventured. 'He'd have been released between twenty and twenty-three months ago. A dog from Spain.'

'Oh,' the girl said, staring. 'I wouldn't have been here then. You'd best ask Mrs Vinicombe. You should find her at the farm.'

So, turning the car, Tim drove back down the lane.

Mrs Vinicombe was old, indeed very old, but clearly with all her wits about her.

'Oh,' she said after Tim had explained his mission. 'I really don't see how I can help you if you don't even know the girl's surname. A lot of people pass through here, you know. One can't remember them all.'

'We do realize that,' Phoebe apologized, 'and we're very sorry to bother you, but it really is important. Tim here's a vet in a practice in Somerstrand. Show her your papers, Tim. And there's been a small outbreak there,' she went on talking as he brought them out, 'of a particularly nasty tropical disease that we strongly suspect was passed on by a Spanish dog quarantined here. One man has actually died.'

'I see.' An uneasy expression flickered over Mrs Vinicombe's wrinkled face. 'You'd better come in. Sit down,' she went on, leading the way into a dark, unlived-in room with heavy furniture, the kind of room perhaps best described as a parlour. Going over to a tall, glass-fronted cupboard, she pulled out two thick green hardbacked volumes. 'The register,' she explained. 'Well, whatever this dog's been up to, he won't have had the chance to spread anything here. We're much too careful.' With what Phoebe recognized as a faintly defensive air, she demanded, 'And what disease would that be? Whatever it is, it must have an incubation period of over six months.'

'It can have,' Tim told her. 'In this case it must have had. It's called Primmer's disease, if that means anything to you.'

Rather surprisingly it did, if not in the sense that Tim had intended. The effect on Mrs Vinicombe was dramatic.

'Oh!' she exclaimed. 'That!' Going swiftly out of the room, she called up the nearby staircase, 'Marion! Can you come down for a minute?'

'Coming!' returned a voice from somewhere above them and seconds later a middle-aged woman with a refined and, Tim suspected, permanently anxious face appeared in the doorway.

'My daughter,' the old woman explained. 'Marion, do you remember Mr Thompson telling us about a telephone call they had at the surgery two or three months ago? More probably two. From somewhere up north. From a young woman whose dog we'd had here, which was why she picked on our vet, thinking he'd have more contact with foreign animals than the average one in the community. He couldn't help, though; he hadn't any of the drugs needed for whatever was affecting her dog. Wasn't that called Primmer's disease? I'm pretty sure it was.'

'Yes, it was,' confirmed Marion, showing more animation now. 'But Mr Thompson thought she must have got the name wrong and was probably confusing it with canine leishmaniasis, which does occur in Spain, whereas Primmer's was an African thing.' Marion was certainly blessed with an excellent memory. 'What is it? Why are you looking at each other like that?'

'Because you've just solved at least part of our mystery.' Tim explained the situation. 'We knew the dog from Spain had fought with a Somerstrand poodle, which has since succumbed after presumably infecting its owner, the dead man, but there was still the possibility that the poodle might have picked up the bug from some other source. But now you've told us that the Spanish dog has in fact developed the disease, that rather wipes out any doubt, wouldn't you say?'

Both Vinicombes agreed that they would.

'It's quite baffling that a dog born and bred in Spain should have developed something which, as your Mr Thompson said, should occur only in Africa,' Tim went on, 'but there just has to be some individual link that we're unlikely to discover. In any case, it's no longer a question of whether or not it could have happened. It did.'

'So then why do you need now to trace this girl?' The old woman was beginning to show the effect of all these minor shocks. 'She knows what's wrong with her dog, and she must be getting veterinary advice.'

'Because the Somerstrand outbreak, small as it is, is causing an absolute furore there,' Phoebe explained. 'If only we could convince the locals that we know the cause of it and can therefore, one hopes, contain it, everybody might just possibly calm down.'

'We'd never dream of revealing her name,' persisted Tim, with one silent reservation, 'but I really should very much like to talk to her. It could be a great help, you know.'

Mrs Vinicombe and her daughter eyed each other doubtfully.

'After all, he is a vet,' Marion said persuasively. 'It wouldn't be like giving information to just anyone.'

Her mother supposed it wouldn't.

'Well, we can but try. Do you know the breed of this dog? Or what it was called?'

'A smallish golden-brown mongrel, we gather,' Phoebe answered, 'and for some reason the Spanish *au pair* girl at the house he visited called him "Seed", though the boy there, the son of the man who died, thought it wasn't his real name.'

'"Seed",' Marion echoed. 'Oh, Cid. El Cid. Rodrigo. It has to be that.'

'Good girl,' said her mother much more brightly. 'I remember Rodrigo now. Nice little thing. Oh dear, that's very sad. It must be quite a while since he left.'

'A little under two years, we reckon,' supplied Tim.

'Wait a minute, though,' Phoebe put in. 'Is it really necessary to go through all this? You don't think your Mr Thompson would remember the girl's name? We can tell him it's Clare, for a start. That could help.'

'I doubt it.' Marion shook her head. 'I don't think he took the call himself. I'm sure it was somebody else. No, we ought to be able to dig it out of the records.'

'Around two years then,' the old woman repeated. 'Right.' Casting aside one of her volumes, she started upon the second, running a finger swiftly down each page. 'Oh yes,' she said at last. 'Here it is. Clare Forrester. And in view of everything I suppose you'd better have her address too. What we have here is 30 Lauderdale Avenue, Moreton-in-Marsh. I'll write it down for you. And the telephone number. And I'd be very interested to hear the outcome.'

'You most certainly shall,' Tim said with a deep sigh of relief. 'That's a promise.'

'I thought she said this Clare Forrester made the call from somewhere up north,' worried Phoebe, as they started back for home. 'But Moreton-in-Marsh isn't, surely? I thought it was somewhere near Stratford-upon-Avon.'

'It is,' he agreed. 'But this could be her parents' address. If she was in Spain for some time, as she must have been, to have a dog there, she'd have needed some base in the UK from where she could be contacted. Anyway, at least it's given us a starting point. Bit of a battleaxe, that Mrs Vinicombe, didn't you think?'

Phoebe did. 'Though you must need to be tough in a job like that. It was the daughter I was rather sorry for, so obviously under Mum's thumb. But it was clever of her to work out the dog's name like that. I was a bit slow there.'

For a while they drove on in a companionable silence broken eventually by Phoebe.

'Once we've got to the bottom of all this, assuming that we do, how do we go about trying to cool things in Somerstrand?'

'It's early to say.' He slowed down to avoid startling two little girls on ponies who were taking up more than their fair share of the narrow road. 'There's no way anyone can guarantee that no further cases will crop up. But we really must try to contact this Forrester girl. For all we know, all hell could be breaking loose wherever she is. Or not, of course.

Either way it would be some kind of marker for us down here.'

'And what's going to happen to poor old Ivy?' Ellen had told Phoebe about her. 'She won't die, will she?'

'No, I'm sure it won't come to that, but the next few months won't be much fun for her. Endless trips to Bristol and total ostracism in Jubilee Crescent.'

He glanced at his watch. They had spent longer at Underdown Farm than he had been reckoning on. Phoebe saw and misinterpreted the look.

'Wouldn't it be a good idea to stop somewhere for a cup of tea? I don't know about you, but I could use one.'

'All right, I suppose so,' he agreed reluctantly. 'Keep a lookout for somewhere, then. I seem to remember there's a transport café a bit further on along this road.'

'Transport café? I thought this was meant to be a pleasant afternoon out!'

'It was,' he told her rather testily. 'But it won't be if we waste much more time. Look, I can see the sign to it – "Café".'

He was right. Swinging the car into the small park in front of the prefabricated erection, he hustled her into a strictly utilitarian snack bar, saw her onto a battered seat with a torn rexine cover and rushed over to the counter.

'I was hoping to keep this as more of a surprise for you,' he said on his return, a cup and saucer in each hand. 'I take it you don't want anything to eat? No? But from the look of you I think I'd better come clean now.'

'I think you had.' Phoebe took her cup. 'Thanks.'

'Well,' aware that apart from one old man in a corner, they were the only customers, Tim dropped his voice, 'the Crook thinks it's time we got married.'

'The Crook does?' The cup came into perilously sharp contact with its saucer. 'Why, precisely? And what's it to do with him anyway?'

'No, no, no.' He put a hand over her free one. 'I'm putting this badly. It's not at all what I suppose you're thinking and in any case, just for the record, I made that quite clear to him.' At the recollection he suppressed a smile. 'No, the thing is that his godmother died recently and left him a cottage in Waterbury.'

'His godmother?' She stared at him, the idea of the Crook ever having had a godmother striking her as quite bizarre.

'Yes. I can remember her vaguely, as a matter of fact. She was a widow when I was quite small, no children, a game old thing who went in for growing prize marrows. Mum used to get together with her occasionally. Anyway, she'd been in an old people's home for quite a while, but had flatly refused to sell the cottage because she couldn't bring herself to accept that she'd never go back.'

As he warmed to his theme his voice rose, catching the attention of the proprietress, whose apparent preoccupation with her tea urn failed to deceive Phoebe.

'Watch it,' she warned. 'We have an interested audience.'

'Sorry!' Tim was annoyed with himself. 'Well, the thing is that the Crook and his wife are getting a bit long in the tooth to want to bother about doing it up, as they'd have to to sell it easily, so they're offering to let us have it at a very low cost, bearing in mind that we'd have to work quite hard to make it really habitable. He said there was no need for a mortgage; we could have it on a kind of hire-purchase arrangement, paying him what we would have done for our respective flats until we reached the agreed sum. All legally drawn up and watertight, of course.'

Phoebe was staggered.

'It's not like the Crook to be so accommodating, is it? Have you seen this place? What's it like?'

'Yes, I have, inside and out. The key's in my pocket and if we get a move on you can be looking over it in about half an hour.'

Waterbury, which took its name from a point at one end where two rivulets converged to form a moderate-sized stream, was no more than a hamlet, a cluster of houses all on the same side of the road, backed by a range of low hills, neat fields on the lower slopes, conifers higher up. On the other side of the road the terrain was wilder, rough and uneven, brambles overhanging the deep ditch that formed the larger rivulet's course.

The cottage, at right angles to the road, presented a blank and unrevealing side to passers-by. It was only when they went through the garden gate and up the path that Phoebe could see what it was really like. She contemplated it in silence for some time.

'It's rather jolly, isn't it?' she said eventually. 'That rough grey stone and those quaint little windows. How old do you think it is?'

'Early eighteenth-century, I'm told. Let's go in and take a look. It smells pretty frightful, I must warn you.'

There he was right. It would take an almighty spring-clean to banish the thick dust that had collected on such furniture as remained, to clear the cobwebs from the filthy window panes and deep sills, to freshen the musty atmosphere.

'Maybe it's a good thing to see it at its worst,' he ventured. 'So that we know from the start what we're up against. It is going to be the start, isn't it?'

His appealing gaze and the lock of hair that had flopped over one eye made him look suddenly boyish.

'Oh, I hope so,' said Phoebe enthusiastically. 'I like it, don't you? Much more fun than some little modern bungalow, even if less easy to run. It's got character. Look at that deep stone fireplace. It's quite a big room too, with that bit running back alongside the chimney breast.'

The kitchen was primitive, with a cracked white sink, battered old solid fuel stove and several roughly painted wooden cupboards. Cooking could have played no great part in the life of the Crook's godmother.

'I like the floor.' She looked approvingly at the red quarry tiles, superficially dirty but showing little sign of wear. 'Easy to keep clean.'

'All right so long as you don't drop anything. Still, we can throw down the odd strategic mat.'

Upstairs the two bedrooms were in keeping with the rest of the cottage, both with pleasant views of the hills behind, but the real bonus was the bathroom, which had been modernized to the fullest extent that the building would allow.

'From here it would take us about twenty minutes to get to Somerstrand,' Phoebe calculated as Tim locked up and prepared to head for home. 'One can't complain about that.' A couple of miles further on she added, 'There couldn't be any catch in this, could there, Tim? No hidden horrors – polluted water or constant power cuts, say? You really do trust the Crook?'

'Oh yes. And you know my mama. Her spies would have picked up any hidden snag, believe me; she's already had a whole day to get onto it. The Crook's inclined to be cantankerous and puts on a show of eccentricity when it suits him, but he's pretty good at heart. You should have seen how decent he was with poor old Ivy when she came to tell us about Fritz.'

With a sigh of contentment he drew up at his own door.

'No surgery tonight, praise the Lord. Do we want to eat out or would we rather stay here and make plans? There's plenty of food in the fridge.'

'Definitely make plans.'

'Wonderful. And there's also a bottle of champagne in the icebox. I've been hoping for the last twenty-four hours that it might acquire an occasion to fit it.'

'Perfect. Just one thing.' She took off her jacket and hesitated a moment before saying, 'I hate to strike a pessimistic note, but before we go right over the moon have you considered the possibility of your coming unstuck with the Crook? In which case we might find a remote country cottage a bit of a millstone. If we go ahead with this, you don't think we could be getting in too deep?'

'No, I don't.' Now he was washing his hands and fetching out the Snoopy apron she had given him at Christmas. 'You for one are no way going to lose your job, and modesty forbids me to repeat what the Crook said to me yesterday about my veterinary talents!'

'Come off it!' she ordered. 'Don't be so tantalizing. What did he say? Tell me.'

‘Well,’ he reached up to the shelf where the glasses reserved for special occasions were kept, ‘that in spite of my sometimes regrettable flippancy I was generally reliable, hard-working and conscientious. And that the locals, or at least most of them, thought pretty highly of me, and that I’d acquitted myself very well so far in the present little drama.’

‘Gorblimey!’ She could hardly believe her ears. ‘It’s true enough, I know, but coming from the Crook . . . Let’s pray he never discovers our guilty secret!’

‘He won’t,’ said Tim confidently and kissed her.

30

With the possible exception of Patrick, nobody at the Edenfield house slept much during the night following the burglary. Clare tossed and turned till the early hours, her overactive brain refusing to give up on the question of how best to deal with Jane, not to mention what she was going to do about Bill Foster's offer. Paul, who had been afraid he might oversleep, found himself at least six inches too long for the sofa, which had never been intended to do duty as a bed. Anne's watering eyes and continuous yawns told their own tale, leading Clare to suspect that she was in a state of mild shock that might well prove a problem in store for Alison.

It was a relief to see Paul and his car safely out of sight some minutes before Jane and the girl from the cattery were due, but it distressed her to have to press the children to leave for school at their usual time.

'You know what the detective said,' she reminded Anne. 'Everything must seem as normal as possible.'

'Then what about you? You aren't leaving at your normal time!'

'Well, I can't, can I, not if I've got to have some kind of conversation with Jane. Besides there's the date at the police station. I'll have to tell her I need to see Mr Charters, which means going to his house, and not too early, as he's ill.'

'It sounds pretty sneaky to me.' Patrick scowled.

'Of course it's sneaky!' she returned in exasperation. 'But you know the score. What else can I do?'

Jane and the other girl arrived at the same moment, apparently without having made contact.

Melanie Simpson was thin, dark, bespectacled and, to judge from her solemn manner, probably humourless, while at the same time giving the impression of entire reliability. Clare didn't anticipate any great rapport between her and Jane, nor, it was patently obvious, did Jane.

After greeting them Clare explained, 'In the end I didn't write out any details for Melanie. I can leave a bit late this morning, as I've realized I'll have to go to see my boss at his home and you can tell her anything I've forgotten, can't you?'

'Oh right,' answered Jane, slightly surprised and went off to take in the first of the day-dogs, leaving Clare to tell the newcomer about feeding arrangements, in what order to let the inmates out from their runs into the paddock and which potential fighters had to be kept apart.

Other than still looking somewhat battered, Jane was just as ever – casual, offhand, adept at putting the minimum effort into anything she had to do. Clare's near certainty that she knew nothing about the burglary hardened into conviction when she observed the total fascination with which she kept eyeing Melanie.

'Weirdo, isn't she?' she commented when the other girl was out of earshot. 'Can't you just see her in a Sally Army bonnet?'

Clare waited to see Jane cross the yard before ringing the office – from Alison's bedroom, but even so the extension below that was used for business purposes was wide open to would-be eavesdroppers.

Sybil was far from happy to hear how late she expected to be.

'Oh Clare, do you really have to? You couldn't have hit on a worse day. Mrs Charters and the accountant are coming in this morning to talk to us all. We don't know why, but it must be important. Why Mrs Charters, I ask you?'

'Presumably because Mr isn't up to it. Yes, I see it's unfortunate, but I've fixed to go to the police to make a statement about a fairly dramatic burglary here last night.'

'How dramatic?' Sybil's gasp of astonishment came clearly over the line. 'Did they get anything?'

'No. Well, only temporarily. I'll tell you all about it later on.'

'You couldn't alter the time you're going to the police?'

'Not really. Other people are going there too. I could have done if I'd known sooner, but it's a bit late now.'

'We only heard this morning,' Sybil lamented. 'She rang about ten minutes ago. I've been on the lookout for you ever since.'

'I really am sorry,' Clare apologized. 'It's a pain. I'll ring Mrs Charters later; she'll have to understand. Meanwhile you just try to remember everything that's said. And the best of luck.'

The two men were already at the police station when she arrived, sitting with Robinson in a little interview room. Foster had already made and signed his statement; now it was for Paul and her to go through a repeat performance of their narratives of the previous night.

'No need to see you separately,' Robinson explained affably. 'Not since the facts are so conclusive. And by the way, your theory was right; the accused is your Harold Clitheroe's brother, though he's determined not to admit that Harold put him up to it. No great virtue in that, of course; it wouldn't help him and Harold would certainly deny it.'

'But he must have admitted that Harold told him about the cash?' said Clare.

'Oh yes; not much point in doing anything else, but according to him it was all in the course of casual conversation. We'll do our best to pin it on Harold, but whether we'll succeed is quite another matter.' He looked at Clare. 'Now what about this Jane girl? How did she seem this morning?'

'Perfectly normal. She has to have told Harold about the pugs and the money, but I'm sure quite genuinely in the course of conversation. What's more, she was so intrigued by a rather odd-looking girl we managed to rope in to help fill a one-day gap that when she first saw her this morning she couldn't take her eyes off her. I can't believe she'd have behaved like that if she'd had any worries connected with last night.'

Robinson nodded.

'Interesting. No, I'm inclined to agree. Still, we'll have to talk to her. Now about this Harold Clitheroe, Mr Foster. When's he returning from Spain, do you know?'

Foster thought for a moment.

'Tomorrow night, I think. Yes, that's right.'

Robinson made a note on the pad in front of him.

'Saturday night. And can you give me his address?'

'Not offhand, but I'll ring it through to you from the office. I'm on my way there now.'

Already late for an appointment, Paul rushed off without stopping to talk, leaving the other two on the steps outside the police station.

'The Edenfields will be back tomorrow,' Clare told Foster. 'Alison rang just after you'd left last night.'

'That's a relief. Not that it will be a very pleasant homecoming for them. I'll be ringing them, of course, but perhaps meanwhile you could tell Rupert that, come what may, I shan't be keeping Clitheroe on after this. And by the way, Clare, my offer to you stands. You seem to have just the qualifications we need, apart from being a stalwart support in a crisis.'

He grinned. She beamed back.

'Well, I can tell you right now I couldn't be more pleased.'

Harold Clitheroe wasn't the only one about to face unemployment, she discovered as soon as she entered the Charters' office. Nobody was working. Sybil and Anna were the only people in sight, sitting at Anna's desk over cups of instant coffee. They both looked stunned.

'Well?' Clare demanded.

'They've just left,' Sybil told her. 'Mrs C. and the accountant, that is. You've missed them by a whisker. She was very understanding about you, not that it matters a toss to her any more because from now on her hubby is right out of it. They've sold the business to some big firm in Sunderland – Gordon Sims and Somebody. It doesn't ring any bell with me, but it seems they have a lot in common with us, apart from being bigger and tougher and more with it. At least that was the implication.'

'Ah.' Clare pulled over a third chair and sank onto it. 'But surely all this is due to Charters's health problems, not our inefficiency?'

'No, it's his health all right, poor old thing,' said Anna. 'Heart trouble, not to be monkeyed about with. But what does that do for us? The result's the same. And what gets me most is the way he played it all so close to his chest. A thing like this can't have been fixed up overnight.'

'That's business for you.' Sybil fished in her bag for an aspirin. 'Anyway they want to keep the three of us on – you, Clare, Anna and me – for a few weeks so that you can get them introduced to our Spanish contacts and we can put them in the picture over the paperwork. Anna and I should get redundancy pay, as we've been here over two years, but you'll fall just short of that, won't you?'

'Just.' Clare shrugged. 'Oh well, it can't be helped. What about Barnet?'

'He's for the chop too; they've got their own executives. He's gone off somewhere looking like thunder and didn't say when he'd be back. So it's bye-bye Barcelona for Barnet.'

Sybil's penchant for him had faded since finding out about the Spanish-speaking girlfriend.

'So if he's not here when somebody rings up, what am I meant to do?' Clare asked. 'Did he say?'

'Not a word. I'll get you some coffee.' Sybil stood up. 'Just stall them till he does come back, I reckon, if that's all you can manage. Otherwise carry on as normal. One thing they did stress was that it's got to be business as usual till we're told to the contrary.'

Until Barnet did return, shortly after lunch, there had been no significant calls. Clare caught a brief glimpse of him as she came out of her room in search of a file, but he scuttled hastily off in an unconvincing attempt to pretend he had no idea she was there.

Their first contact came when he strode in to say that there was a call for her. Personal, he added disagreeably.

Melanie's clipped little voice was under strict control, but Clare could sense that it was costing her.

'Clare? I'm extremely sorry to have to ring you at work. Jane gave me your number. The thing is, she's been attacked. They've taken her to hospital.'

'At work, do you mean?'

'Yes. Two young men. They came here asking for her.'

'Is she badly hurt?'

'Not dangerously, but they made an awful mess of her face. I shouldn't be surprised if her nose is broken.'

Clare glanced at her watch – half-past three. Patrick and Anne would be home soon; she had to try to get there first.

'All right, Melanie. Of course you had to ring. I'll be with you as fast as I can, in about half an hour with luck.'

Barnet was in his room, gnawing at a pencil and doing precious little else as far as she could see. He listened impassively to her story.

'Very unfortunate. Still, after this morning I wonder you bothered to come in at all. No doubt they'll be glad to give you a permanent job at that dog place, which is probably as well, as things are.'

'I have been offered a permanent job, as it happens,' she answered sweetly. 'Not at the dog place. In quite a big firm where I'll be doing much the same kind of work as I've been doing here.'

His expression on hearing this made up quite a lot for all he had put her through.

Melanie was enormously relieved to see her. So were the children, who had already arrived. Anne, still looking much the worse for wear, was making a valiant attempt to lend a hand with the evening feeds.

'What happened?' Clare demanded. 'Tell me everything.'

'I was in the office washing bowls,' Melanie recalled. 'A little after two, it would have been. Jane was cleaning out runs. And then these two young men arrived, rather low types, I thought; scruffy, in their twenties. One of them asked me if I was Jane, and the other said no, not me, I couldn't possibly be.'

The angry flush that suffused the plain little face left little doubt as to the kind of reason he had given for this opinion.

'So I called Jane and she came. They were a horrible pair, but it never occurred to me that they were going to be violent. Anyway, they said a lot of very nasty things to her, called her every name I'd heard and a whole lot more besides, and then they both started hitting her about the face.'

'With anything?'

'No, just their fists, but it was enough. I yelled at them, but of course that didn't do any good. So . . .'

'So?'

'So,' the words came out in a rush, 'I took the fire extinguisher from the office and squirted them both in the face. And after that they weren't able to do any more. Just ran off rubbing their eyes and screeching. They never thought I'd do anything, I suppose. They thought I was just – well . . .'

Another blush.

'Then they were wrong, weren't they?' Clare said admiringly. 'And after that you rang for an ambulance?'

'Yes. And the police. The ambulance came first, but they followed it to the hospital.'

'But why had they got it in for Jane, if they didn't even know her?' Patrick wanted to hear.

'I couldn't understand that. They seemed to think she'd shopped – that was the word they used – a friend of theirs, at least he must have been a friend, called Brian. But she didn't know what they were talking about either. She kept screaming at them that they'd got it all wrong and that she didn't know anyone called Brian. It didn't make any difference, though. They just kept on hitting her until . . .'

She paused.

'You let them have it. I wonder how long it will take for them to be caught.'

'I think they may need to go to a doctor,' Melanie offered pensively.

'M'm. And if they're friends of this Brian . . .'

'But Brian's a very ordinary name.'

'Yes, but we know who this one is.' Catching Melanie's look of sheer amazement, she went on, 'In fact I think it's time you heard the whole story. It can't matter now.'

The upshot was that Clare, being back so much earlier than usual, made them all a high tea and Melanie, looking happier, stayed on for it and heard everything.

'I suppose I'd better go along to the hospital and try to see Jane,' Clare said as they finished. 'I'm sure that's what your mother would do.'

'Think she'll be pleased to see you?' Patrick still couldn't quite get over the tactics that had been used on Jane.

'I shouldn't think so, but all the same it would look pretty callous if I didn't.'

'You're not going out this evening?' Anne nearly dropped the plate she was carrying over to the sink. 'Oh, you can't! What if they come back?'

'They won't.' Melanie's tone was dry. 'Certainly not tonight. Still, if you're worried, why don't I stay here till Clare gets back?'

Anne thought that a very good idea.

'Yes,' her brother agreed. 'And then we can play Monopoly. No more homework till September.'

Next day would be the last of the term.

'Another thing I've been wondering about,' Melanie went on. 'I shouldn't think Jane will be able to work for quite a while. Not tomorrow anyway. So if you like, I could probably get the other girl at the cattery, whose day off it will be, to stand in for me while I come here again. If I let her have my free one next week, she'll get two running, which she'll probably quite like. Shall I ring and ask her? I know her home number.'

Clare was only too glad to accept the offer.

'But even so, I think I'll stay here too. The police may well come up here wanting to take you off the job to answer more questions.'

She would ring Mrs Charters about it direct, she decided, and then just notify Barnet. Foster's offer had given her the first lift she had had in weeks.

At the hospital nobody objected to her seeing Jane, whom

she found in a ward containing a dozen reasonably healthy looking patients and several other people taking advantage of the evening visiting hour. As she anticipated, the younger girl was far from pleased to see her.

'What are you doing here?' she demanded, glowering at Clare through one partially closed and very swollen eye. The other was covered by a pad, as was the bridge of her nose.

'What do you think?' Clare dumped a bottle of grapefruit squash, hastily pilfered from Alison's larder, on the bedside locker. 'We were all horrified at what happened to you. How do you feel?'

'Well, just take a look and guess.'

'Yes, but have they given you any painkillers?'

'Oh yeah, a couple of pills. They helped for a bit but they're wearing off now.' She gave Clare another hostile look. 'I don't know how you could've done it. Bloody police spy!'

There wasn't much point in prevaricating.

'I didn't do it exactly voluntarily, you know. The detective who came round last night was determined I shouldn't say anything to you about the burglary. I suppose I could have gone to work without seeing you, but then there was Melanie to deal with. There wasn't any time to write her a note last night, I can tell you.' She paused for breath. 'And on the credit side, the way you behaved made it pretty obvious that you couldn't know anything about it and I was able to tell the police so.'

'What d'you mean, the way I behaved?'

'Well, the way you were so fascinated by Melanie's appearance. Sally Army, remember? It wasn't exactly the remark of somebody anxious about what happened the night before.

'Huh!' Jane's expression became slightly less belligerent. 'That Melanie, I must say she was good. By the time she'd finished with them they must've been hurting as much as I was. Who's this Brian then, do you know?'

'Your Harold's brother. You didn't realize that?'

'No, I never.' Jane opened her mouth wide in amazement, found the movement too painful and closed it again. 'I knew he had a brother somewhere but I never met him. I don't think he ever mentioned his name.'

'They say he's a crook with several convictions. Harold must have known that and put him up to it. At the very least he would have realized what Brian was likely to do, with the Edenfields away like that.'

'Oh, Lor'!' Jane looked so appalled that Clare considered fetching a nurse. 'And all because I told him about that cash.'

'Yes, we did realize it must have been you, but it didn't follow that you'd have any idea what he'd do about it.'

'The rotten sod!' said Jane bitterly. 'Course I didn't realize. Bloody good thing I finished with him.'

'You did? When?'

'The night before last. We had a good old barney, see. He was mucking around on the side with some other girl and had the gall to tell me he couldn't decide which one to go steady with. So I made up his mind for him, didn't I? But that was all after I'd told him about the lolly. Pity.'

That Clare could hardly dispute.

'The cash has been recovered, that's one good thing, but this hasn't done much for your beauty. How long are they keeping you in, do you know?'

'They weren't sure. A few days probably. They don't think there's any serious damage, but they didn't like the idea of me living alone in this state. Harold never moved in, by the way, and if he had he'd be out on his ear pronto.'

'Poor old Jane.' Clare sighed. 'You'll have to be a bit more particular next time. Oh, I haven't told you – Alison's coming back on Saturday and Melanie's going to help out again tomorrow.'

'Oh yeah?' A faintly guilty look penetrated Jane's bruises. 'Well, I don't think I'll be going back there any more, not after all this. I just couldn't fancy it. Maybe I'll go down south and stay with my sister for a while. Alison shouldn't have much trouble finding someone else, not with all the school leavers who'll be looking for work from any day now.'

'That's true.' From Jane such a show of concern was surprising. 'So am I forgiven?'

'I suppose so.' Jane did her best to make a grimace and winced. 'Thanks for the grapefruit anyway.'

Back at the Edenfield house Clare found the other three quite happily absorbed in their Monopoly and it was quite a while before Melanie left, after wanting to hear about Jane.

'Anything from the police?' Clare asked.

'Oh yes,' Patrick told her. 'That Robinson man rang. Mel's going along some time tomorrow to look at mugshots.'

'"Mel",' quoted Clare, after running her home in the car, a brief desertion which Anne had to accept. 'Sounds as if you'd got on all right!'

'Oh yes.' Patrick sounded rather smug as he collected up the Monopoly bits and pieces. 'I'm arranging for her to see a beautician.'

'You're *what?*'

'Yes. She was very upset by what that pervert said to her, you know.'

'That's what I thought. So what exactly did he say? She wasn't going to tell me.'

'It wasn't actually to her. It was about her in front of her. He said she was a scraggy little runt with a tiny trap and eyes like dried currants.'

Small wonder that Melanie had wielded the fire extinguisher.

'So then I remembered that one of the blokes at school had an older sister who looked very much like Mel. I've seen her quite often at school dos. She went to this beautician, they said, which was why she suddenly started to look quite decent. So I promised Mel I'd find out the name for her.'

'And he actually got away with it?' Clare breathed to Anne after staring at him in silence for a long time. 'How old is he now? Fifteen? What's he going to grow up into, I'd like to know!'

Anne shrugged.

'A shrink, I should think,' she said simply.

31

Tim had been right in his surmise that the Moreton-in-Marsh address was that of Clare Forrester's parents, but he could never have anticipated the problem he would have in establishing direct contact with her. Knowing nothing of how shaken they had been by their daughter's account of the burglary at the kennels and subsequent attack on Jane, he was disconcerted to find that no way was Mrs Forrester going to give Clare's telephone number to any strange young man, however agreeable he might sound and whatever he might claim as his profession.

'Why don't you just write to her at this address?' she asked him. 'I'd send the letter straight on to her.'

'Because it would take much longer and it really is rather urgent.'

'In what way urgent?'

Oh dear, thought Tim. How could he begin to explain to her the rumours that still abounded in Somerstrand, that more perfectly healthy pets had been destroyed, and that Dr Graylaw was being driven to near distraction by a spate of fearful patients complaining about the most trivial disorders?

'Well, my main concern is that little Spanish dog of hers.'

'Yes? How do you come to know anything about that?'

'It's a long story, difficult to condense. Well, there's been a small outbreak down here of a particularly nasty parasitic foreign disease and after quite a bit of amateur detective work, far too involved to relate over the telephone, we think we've managed to trace it back to him. I'll gladly write it all to you if you'd like, but meanwhile would you mind telling me what has happened to him? We did gather that he must be very ill.'

'Yes, I'm afraid he's dead and it was the kind of disease you mention. My daughter was heartbroken after all she's been through getting him back from Spain. Oh dear, if you're right that's quite dreadful. But he wasn't in your part of the world for more than a few hours. She was just dropping in on a friend. Surely not . . ?'

'I'm afraid it looks very like it, Mrs Forrester,' Tim said diffidently. 'Because we gather that during those few hours he had a fight, probably not started by him, with another dog who subsequently developed it. That's one way the parasite can be passed on, you see. Er – your daughter's all right, is she? Physically, I mean?'

'Why?' June Forrester's tone sharpened. 'Is there any reason why she shouldn't be? Humans don't get it, do they?'

That put Tim right on the spot.

'You didn't realize that? I'm afraid they can, if precautions aren't taken. Hasn't she had a blood test?'

'Not as far as I know. She's never said anything about it to us.'

'Perhaps she didn't want to worry you. If the illness was properly diagnosed, I'm sure she would have been tested.'

It was at this point that June Forrester capitulated.

'All right, I'll give you her number, Mr – er – Proud. She won't be at home for the next couple of days, but when you do get her would you mind asking her to ring us as soon as possible?'

Those last two days at the kennels passed swiftly for Clare. Pam returned to work the morning after the wedding, breezy and eager to recount all the details, but anything she had to tell fell flat in comparison with the events she had missed. Once again Melanie failed visibly to impress and for the first time it occurred to Clare that Patrick might after all have something rather more than mere precocity in his insight into her problems.

'I know Pam's a lot older than you,' she murmured to her in a quiet moment, 'but can you picture her doing what you did with that fire extinguisher? I think we're going to have to train you to be a bit more self-assertive!'

It was quite heart-warming to see the effect this had on Melanie's tiny trap.

Then halfway through the afternoon she was borne off in a police car to look, not at mugshots, but at the actual mugs themselves, as a triumphant Patrick put it later on.

'They said it wasn't hard to catch up with them,' Melanie explained. 'All they had to do was go down to that Brian's flat and ask the neighbours about his associates. They weren't at all popular, any of them, and their bloodshot eyes gave them away completely. It's hard to understand how anyone could be quite so stupid, coming here openly in broad daylight, don't you think?'

Clare did. 'Too much lunchtime beer, maybe. Or drugs.'

At last, on the Saturday evening, Rupert and Alison arrived home by taxi, he managing his crutches remarkably well and she looking quite fit and brown in spite of all the recent strain.

'Something's happened, hasn't it?' she demanded after embracing everyone. 'You're all bottling something up. And what's the matter with you, Anne? You shouldn't be looking so rough on the first day of the holidays. And oh dear, I forgot all about Pam's day off, didn't I? That's been haunting me all the way home. Whatever did you do about it?'

Clare answered that one.

'Well, actually that's where we struck lucky, in a funny kind of way. But I think it's Anne who should tell you all about it. Look, I'm just going to make sure that everyone's safely battened down and then I'll be back.'

When she returned a good twenty minutes later Anne was noticeably less tense and her parents almost at a loss for words.

'It's beyond belief,' Alison managed to say. 'And wouldn't it just have to happen while Rupert and I were away!'

'That could have been part of the reason why it did,' Clare said. 'Of course Mr Foster turning up like that gained us quite a lot of precious time. And by the way, Rupert, he's offered me a job in his office, just as everything's folding up in mine. That really is a bit of luck.'

'Oh, of course,' Alison recalled. 'You said something about conditions there the other day while he was here. Well, I do promise you that you couldn't have found anyone better to work for.'

'And he's lucky too,' Rupert added gratefully. 'As they say, there's an up side to everything.'

32

It was well after ten that Saturday evening when Clare found herself back in her flat – a relief in many ways but also something of an anticlimax. Everything was suddenly so silent; no barking dogs, no Anne or Patrick going about their usual fairly noisy pursuits, a light coating of dust on the furniture, the fridge iced up, the water unheated, several hastily abandoned pans lying on the draining board crying out for a good scrub, a couple of bills on the mat plus a long, semi-legible scrawl from an elderly cousin engaged in perpetual strife with her younger and rowdier neighbours. She considered telephoning Paul, who had probably been trying to get through to her all evening, then abandoned the idea. The way she was feeling, a long conversation would be altogether too much of an effort. Even so, she was not to be spared.

'Oh Clare, at last you're back.' Her mother sounded quite untypically agitated. 'I couldn't contain myself any longer. I take it you haven't yet heard from that young man?'

'Paul?'

'No, no, the vet from Somerstrand.'

'Mum, I've no idea what you're talking about.'

'No, of course you couldn't have.' June Forrester was plainly trying to take a pull on herself. 'He was a young man – at least he sounded young – called Proud, and he wanted to talk to you about Rodrigo. He seems to think he must have passed on that illness of his to some dog down there.'

'What?' Clare found herself beginning to tremble. 'How could he have? We were only in Somerstrand for a couple of hours when I looked in on Montse.'

'I know that, but he's got it into his head that there was a dog-fight. Probably not Rodrigo's fault, he did admit.'

'Well, all I can say is that if there was, I didn't know about it. He must have been told that by the Proctors, or rather the little boy. Neither of the parents was there. And Montse hasn't said a thing about it in her letters.'

'I really don't know, dear. He'll have to tell you about it himself. He sounded quite nice, and friendly enough. But what's worrying your father and me is that he says humans can catch the illness. He seemed quite concerned about whether or not you'd had a blood test.'

'I did have one, and it was negative. Nothing can happen now.'

'But you never said anything about it.'

June's sigh of relief came clearly over the line.

'There wasn't much point. You'd only have been worried if I'd told you before it and afterwards it was all water under the bridge. So when do you think this man will ring?'

'Some time tomorrow morning, I imagine. I shan't keep you any longer now because you must be tired after all those nights at that dogs' home. Everything there went smoothly, I take it?'

'Well, relatively, I suppose.'

'And you'll ring tomorrow after this young man has spoken to you? We'll be in all day. Good. Now go to bed as soon as possible and meanwhile try to put all this Rodrigo business out of your mind.'

Some hope, thought Clare, wondering what was coming next.

That Sunday morning Tim, the Crook, Phoebe, Graylaw and Matthew all gathered at Tim's flat to listen in on his call to Clare. Phoebe had been less than happy about allowing Matthew to be there, but he had been so tenaciously insistent on getting Montse's address at the first possible moment that she could scarcely deny him, particularly after all he had been through.

'It means you'll have to watch what you say,' she warned Tim. 'And don't forget that whatever it is will go straight back to his mother.'

Clare's voice was shaky when she answered, shortly after the cup of coffee that had done duty as a late breakfast after an almost sleepless night.

'My mother's already been on to me,' she told Tim, 'but she didn't explain much. All I've gathered is that you've somehow come to hear what happened to my dog and you think he passed on his illness to another one, who has to have been the Proctors', as their house was the only place in Somerstrand where we stopped.'

'That's what it looks like,' said Tim half apologetically, 'and also I fear to Mr Proctor via his own dog. He – er – died last week.'

'Mr Proctor?' Clare's voice, audible to everyone in the room, rose almost to a shriek. 'Rodrigo did that? And I never even realized there was a fight.'

'Well, I can tell you from first-hand experience that the Proctor dog would have fought with almost anything on four legs. And neither of the others realized at the time, any more than you did. It was only after you'd left, according to Matthew, that he and Montse found quite a deep bite mark. Now look,' he went on, rightly attributing Clare's prolonged silence to profound shock, 'we can't totally rule out the possibility that it was the other way round and that the Proctor poodle infected your dog. It's just that it seems wildly unlikely, given that yours had come in from abroad and the Proctor one had never been out of this country. Did your vet tell you the name of the illness, by the way?'

'Yes. It was an African thing called Primmer's disease.'

'That's what we thought.' Tim shot an eloquent glance at the intently listening Crook. 'And as it doesn't occur naturally in Spain it must somehow have been brought in from elsewhere. You never took him anywhere, say a trip to Gibraltar?'

'Heavens, no! But as they reminded me here, there are lots of connections between North Africa and Spain, and one never knows what could come off a cargo ship in Barcelona.'

'True,' agreed Tim, and went on to tell her the Somerstrand snake story, which by this time had gone the rounds. 'Now, as to why I'm ringing you – and don't think we don't realize what a dreadful shock this must have been to you . . .'

'Well, yes, I mean Mr Proctor . . .' Clare, who had never fainted in her life, was beginning to wonder whether she might be about to start, which was where Phoebe, who could hear everything, particularly regretted Matthew's presence. In front of him Tim could hardly explain, however delicately, that Walter's demise was hardly a cause for universal regret.

'It's no good thinking that way,' he said instead. 'It's just one of those freak awful things that do happen through nobody's fault. No, the thing is that in a little place like Somerstrand everyone knows everyone else and gossip spreads like wildfire and, thanks to a pestilential eaves-dropping woman who used to be our surgery cleaner, this business has been blown up out of all proportion.'

'How do you mean, exactly? She's been saying that other people are likely to catch it?' An awful thought struck Clare. 'I take it nobody has? Apart from Mr Proctor, that's to say?'

'Well,' Tim glanced rather desperately at the Crook, who shrugged unhelpfully, 'the Proctors' daily help has, but she won't die; it was caught in time. Incidentally, have you had a blood test, Miss Forrester?'

'Oh yes,' said Clare wearily. 'That was all right, rather surprisingly.'

'And her dog, who has died, I'm afraid.' No point in mentioning the woman from Bath. 'No, what's causing a bit of a furore round here just now is the appearance right out of the blue of a pretty nasty disease that by rights shouldn't crop up in Britain. A lot of the fuss and hysteria could have been avoided if it hadn't been for our wretched, loud-mouthed cleaner and one ambitious schoolboy who managed to get the gutter press in on it.'

'Oh, no!'

'But if we can just get it across to the locals that we now know where it comes from and that it's been contained, with luck the whole thing will,' he was about to say "die a natural death", but hastily amended it to, "fizzle out."

'Oh,' said Clare. 'But how did you manage to find me?'

'Through young Matthew Proctor - he's here now - with a bit of assistance from my fiancée, who used to teach him. And that telephone call you put through about the specific drugs made all the difference. It's quite a saga, actually.'

'I see,' said Clare, who didn't entirely and didn't particularly want to.

'Wait, Tim,' Graylaw interrupted. 'Just ask her if anyone up there has got it.'

'Did you hear that?' Tim asked. 'That's our local doctor. Matthew's father was one of his patients.'

'Yes, I heard. Only one, to my knowledge. My dog bit him because he was semi-assaulting a friend of mine he was fond of. But he isn't going to die either, or so I'm told.'

'And is the dog likely to have infected anyone else?' Graylaw had seized the receiver from Tim. 'Forgive me for butting in, my dear. The last thing we want to do is cause you further distress. It's been a wretched business.'

'Oh, hello,' said Clare. 'No, certainly no other humans. As to animals, that's a thing that will hang in the balance for years, I suppose. I very much doubt it, though.'

'Quite. But at least they're onto it up there. You couldn't give me the names of the vet and the doctor who mostly dealt with it, I suppose?'

'Yes, of course.'

Bolsover and Smethers were not the names she was likely to forget in a hurry, nor their places of work.

'Thanks.' Graylaw's pen scratched over a piece of paper that Tim passed over to him. 'Now shall I put you on to Matthew?'

'But can he bear to speak to me?' She almost cringed at the suggestion.

'Of course he can.' Tim had grabbed back the receiver. 'He remembers you very well, enjoyed meeting you, and above all he wants you to give him Montse's address. That's been quite a thing, I can tell you.'

Phoebe was proud of him for the reassurance he managed to convey without any unseemly candour.

'Is that Matthew?' It cost Clare quite an effort to sound remotely normal. 'I'm so very, very sorry about everything. It was a bad day for your family when I came to see you. You'd like Montse's address, is that it?'

'Oh yes, please,' he said earnestly, accepting the pencil and blank envelope hastily snatched up by Phoebe.

'Then hold on while I look in my book. It's right here. She'll be so glad. She writes to me often and she was very sad when she never heard from you again.'

'That was Daddy's fault.' Matthew's tone got across just about everything Tim had been unable to say. 'Mum was sad about it too. Now perhaps Montse will be able to come over and stay with us.'

'I'm sure she'd love to. Here's the address then. And after that maybe she'll come on up here to see me.'

It was Tim who brought the call, which threatened to become emotional, to a tactful end.

'You've helped us enormously, Miss Forrester. I'm only so extremely sorry it all had to happen. Oh, just one thing,' as a thought struck him, 'you wouldn't have a cat, I suppose?'

'No, at least not for the moment, though I've been thinking about it. Why?'

'No reason,' said Tim hastily, with an expressive look at Phoebe. 'I was just wondering.'

33

By the time Paul arrived that Sunday morning, unheralded and inclined to be anxious about her, Clare was on her sitting-room floor, going through a pile of letters, all in the same un-English hand.

'I didn't ring earlier in case you were having a lie-in. What are you doing down there? You look awful.'

'Going through Montse's letters just to see what I may turn up.'

'Montse?'

'Yes, you know; the girl I used to teach in Spain, the one I looked in on in Somerstrand after getting Rods out of quarantine.'

'Oh, her. The *au pair.* Yes, I know. That looks like quite a correspondence. Why the three piles?'

'To indicate the passage of time. She wrote to me from Somerstrand quite often while I was still in Spain. She was terribly homesick and not sure how to cope with various things that cropped up. And then she went on sending letters after we'd met that time and I'd settled in here. And finally after the bust-up with the Proctors she got herself a job in Barcelona and wrote this third lot.' She pointed. 'I gather she hated Proctor himself, but she had hoped to hear from his wife and the boy. She'd been fond of them. But not a word. And now one sees why. He ditched anything like that.' Suddenly recollecting, she got up, putting the letters on a table. 'Oh, I'm sorry. Of course you don't yet know anything about this.'

'About what? I have grasped that the Proctors were the

people she worked for. But what d'you mean "and now"? Has something happened?'

'Sorry. And how it has! I'm going to make us some fresh coffee and then I'll explain. Meanwhile you read these letters, if you can face it, and see what you make of them.'

Various comments followed her into the kitchen as she hunted round for clean crockery and recharged the percolator.

'I wouldn't call her English exactly brilliant. Doesn't seem to understand present tenses, for one thing.'

'No.' She reached for the sugar and a tin of biscuits. 'I never could get that into her head. She just isn't a natural linguist.'

'Well, she doesn't like Proctor, for a start. What's this she says about him? "Bully-boy." Bit old for that, isn't he?'

'Was, I fear,' said Clare. 'He's dead, thanks to Rodsey and me, it seems. Watch out for that cup. You'll spoil the set.'

'Sorry.' With a clatter he put it down. 'I just feel I've had my ration of shocks for the last few days. So get on and tell me, will you?'

As concisely as she was able, Clare did.

'I feel so shattered,' she confessed. 'Of course it's infinitely worse for the Proctors and that poor daily woman, but it's an appalling thing to have to realize that one's responsible, however indirectly, for someone else's death.'

'Of course I see that.' Paul made a cautious attempt to raise the cup to his lips once more, to find somewhat to his surprise that he could. 'But when you come to think about it, it can't be all that uncommon an experience, and in your case there can't be the remotest shred of blame, no carelessness, nothing. No, what really shakes me is the thought of how easily you yourself might have caught the disease. So what am I meant to be looking for in these lengthy epistles?'

'I don't really know. Some indication as to how Mr Proctor might have caught it from the dog, I suppose. He doesn't sound what you'd describe as an affectionate person. Any details about the onset of symptoms. You know.'

Paul didn't really, But he did his best.

'Part one doesn't – can't – tell us anything significant,' he commented after several minutes of silent reading, 'except that she wasn't very happy in Somerstrand, mainly because Proctor was an exceptionally difficult employer, always picking on her for the slightest reason. The wife and the daily help were obviously kind to her and she was very fond of the boy.'

'Exactly.'

'And the final lot written to you from Spain won't help us, as you say she never heard anything more from the family, so it's the middle ones we've got to concentrate on, written from Somerstrand to you here.'

There was another long pause while letters were passed from one to the other.

'Nothing about symptoms,' she said after a while.

'I shouldn't think she'd have cared a toss about his symptoms, if any.'

'No, and in any case she left so soon after we called to see her that they wouldn't have had much time to show up. Stupid of me not to have remembered that.'

'She didn't like the dog either. She's really quite graphic about him.' Paul's tense expression had given way to one of mild amusement. 'And the dog was jealous of the kitten. Proctor obviously greatly preferred the dog, so could that have led him to make an undue fuss of him – get licked or so on? Oh yes, here we may have something.' He was actually on the verge of smiling. 'Did you read about the electric shock?'

'I'm not sure. Remind me, anyway.'

'Evidently when this Humphrey creature was really annoyed, which was often, he expressed his displeasure by lifting his leg indoors, against just about anything that took his fancy. That was the one thing that made Mrs Proctor angry enough to protest to her husband; usually she took everything lying down in a way Montse's mother would have scorned to do. And on one occasion – here we have it – Humphrey did it on a light switch which resulted in a slight shock to the boy when he went to turn it on. Proctor was furious, with the unfortunate kitten, not the dog. And all this animal psychology, by the way, came from the daily help. Montse's quite a prolific writer, isn't she? So it is conceivable that from time to time, fearing his wife's rare anger, Proctor brought himself to mop up a puddle?'

'Conceivable, I suppose,' Clare agreed. 'But goodness knows I mopped up enough over Rodrigo. He'd have needed to have a cut on his hand, something like that.'

'Or a cat scratch maybe,' said Paul.

34

In Somerstrand the season wore on. The tourist figures were less impressive than the comparable ones for the previous two years, but at the town hall it was felt that this was more likely attributable to the rival attractions of the Costas than the Primmer's disease scare, which was gradually becoming a thing of the past. Reassuring printed notices had appeared in the surgeries of both the local doctors, Mr Cruikshank and that of the Bagthorpe vet. Predictably Andrew Peters had expressed no gratitude for his copy, but one of Tim's spies reported that even so it had been prominently displayed in his waiting-room. Alec Graylaw wrote a restrained letter to *The Somerstrand Gazette* reiterating the information that the parasite responsible had been traced to a briefly visiting dog bound for the north, where the situation had been competently addressed – a word which seemed comparatively recently to have erupted into the nation's vocabulary and which he now used slightly tongue-in-cheek.

With the breaking up of the schools came a temporary lull in the mothers' meetings at their gates and the interest of the press was diverted to new and more colourful stories – a sinking ferry, a suspected radioactive leak at a nuclear power station and a flood of often ill-targeted personally addressed advertisements for a cure for impotence which caused uproar in families the length and breadth of the county and much ribald hilarity at The George and Dragon.

Visibly more robust now and a good deal less diffident in her manner, Ellen took Matthew on the longed-for holiday to Catalonia, where they had a happy reunion with Montse. Tim and Phoebe were regaled with all the details when they dropped in to see them at the cottage, where strenuous DIY activities were in full swing.

'Don't overdo it too much, will you, Phoebe?' Ellen warned. 'You want to look your best on the day.'

Ivy, on treatment complemented by more rest than she had ever enjoyed in her life, slowly improved and at times was caught looking almost cheerful.

'It's personal relations that have really suffered in all this,' Edward Charlton said to his wife. 'I'm not talking about Proctor; it would be hypocrisy to pretend that he was much loss to anybody, least of all his family, but all the petty backbiting that has gone on, mainly about that wretched Ivy Miller, has been a shaker. I must say I've learnt a thing or two about certain members of our congregation. And others.'

There Tim, tolerant as he was, would have agreed with him. There were several people in the town about whom he would never feel quite the same, not that he had felt much about them in the first place, but in any case just now he had far more important matters on his mind.

35

'It was kind of Tim and Phoebe to ask us to their wedding,' said Priscilla four weeks later as she did her best to cram her head into what looked like a befeathered blue muffin. 'Do you know, I really don't think I should have let Eileen talk me into buying this hat.'

There George was in complete agreement, though by now it was too late to do anything about it. What was more, Priscilla was looking unusually tired, almost as tired as he felt, though that was only to be expected after a ten-day visitation from her sister, who had departed only a couple of days before.

'Mr Cruikshank and Tim seem very friendly these days,' his wife went on. 'I saw them and Phoebe in Porter's not so long ago, all deciding which would be the best dinner service for Mr Cruikshank to give them. And I heard him having a good old gossip about the wedding with Tim's mother in the chemist's while she was waiting for a prescription. It really does seem rather extraordinary when you consider how blatantly Mr Cruikshank took the entire credit for all the research those two did over that dreadful illness. Yet Angela told me only yesterday that they both think it's hilarious. I'd have been furious.'

'Then why weren't they?' Frowning, George fumbled with his tie.

'Apparently it's partly because they're so delighted with that cottage – they've done an awful lot of work on it, you know – and partly because this way it's so much more one in the eye for that horrid vet at Bagthorpe. Angela said he wouldn't have been half so annoyed if Tim had got the kudos. Oh, and George . . .'

'Yes?'

'You know we're bound to have to say at least something to that young Mrs Proctor and the boy at the reception. Don't get too friendly with them, will you?'

'Why should I?' He blinked. 'We're old enough to be her parents. She won't want to waste her time with us.'

'I know, but she's going through a difficult time and you can be a bit of a softie when you're sorry for anyone. It's just that I don't think we should risk asking her to the house. Not with Orestes in and out all the time. He's hardly a cat one could fail to recognize.'

'I do see that.' Glancing at his watch – ten minutes before they must leave – George wondered whether a quick fortifying glass of sherry would be too much of a debauchery. 'Still, they could never make us give him back, not even if they wanted to.'

'No, but it's Tim,' Priscilla persisted, struggling to pierce the muffin with a third hatpin. 'Mr Cruikshank may be friendly just now, but I'm sure he could still be pretty awkward, given cause. Really, he must never find out.'

'Well, how in the name of Fortune could he?' George's patience had just about reached its limit. Definitely a glass of sherry. 'The only people who could give Tim away, apart from Phoebe, of course, are you, me and Angela. I know you won't, I'm damned sure she won't and, as for me, I can tell you here and now that if there's any nonsense of that kind from anyone, I shall look 'em straight in the eye and deny everything!'

'That's my George,' said Priscilla with satisfaction, her thoughts unaccountably straying to the dusty old studio portrait of Mildred, now staring severely up from the bottom shelf in the spare-room wardrobe.

Tempora mutantur! Whatever would she have thought?